THE INFINYDON

MC Lorbiecke

God Slayer: Book One

This is a work of fiction. Names, characters, places, and incidents are either the product of the author's imagination or are used fictitiously. Any resemblance to actual persons, living or dead, events, or locales is entirely coincidental.

ISBN: 979-8-218-03949-3

THE

INFINYDON

Mother Nature exacts revenge for humanity's exploitation of the planet Earth. Dr. Evelyn Humbolt is a captivating professor who makes a startling discovery: a shapeshifting specimen that may live eternal.

A primordial leviathan is resurrected and unleashed into the seas on a bloodthirsty mission to exterminate life.

Ominous prophecies haunt a heretic; disturbing premonitions terrorize a fallen priest. A diverse team of researchers is assembled to save humankind, but will they save humanity from extinction, or will the titanic Infinydon trigger the end of life as we know it?

DEDICATION

First and foremost, I am dedicating this book to the love of my life, John Daniel, and my youngest child, Anton Isaac, for it was you who conceived this entire premise. As a family pastime, we enjoy discussing ideas and collaborating, cultivating them into a complex plot, and my husband used his tenacity to chisel it into something viable. I took up the reins and breathed life into the leviathan, and in cooperation, we wrought a primitive idea into a sophisticated storyline.

Secondly, I must thank my in-laws, John and Josie Lorbiecke, for it was you who literally fed us in those lean times while we fought our way through university so we could live and flourish in the future. You two are saints.

Furthermore, I must thank our extended family, who have cheered me on and helped cultivate us into the thinkers that we have become: all my aunts and uncles, including the Longorias, Lyons, Lorbieckes, Aguayos, and the Stiths. All my children: Anton, Emmie, Dominique, Sonya, and JJ, as well as Shawn, Adrian, Jacob, Charity, and Thaddeus.

I also thank our doggy children for making us laugh when things get too serious: Blade Lucius Lex, Cairo Black Wolf, Kirra Little Mouse, and Little Rukia. I wish to thank my author friends and family who have paved the way for me and counseled me on my journey: Sandi Ogle, Noe Longoria, Jenny Bower, and Taylor Dawn.

ACKNOWLEDGMENTS

As an educator, I must thank the two most wonderful teachers: Mrs. Alsup and Mrs. Johnson, for being ever patient and kind. To all my students through the years who encouraged me in the classroom and kept me sharp as I taught fledgling minds.

I dedicate this legacy to the friends and family members who have already passed away: my mother Lisa Longoria, Grandma and Grandpa Longoria, Lyon, Lorbiecke, Aguayo, Uncle Matt, Uncle JD, Aunt Diane, Mike Lippert, and the beloved puppies who have passed: Brutus Tiberius Rex, Zoe, Mojo, Lady, Bugsy, and Killer. There are not enough words to express my gratitude to everyone I want to mention, but if you have helped and supported me on this journey or are reading this book, I extend my sincere thanks to you.

TABLE OF CONTENTS

1	Beginning of the End	Pg # 13
2	Dominion	Pg # 25
3	The Professor	Pg # 33
4	Specter	Pg # 59
5	Tasmanian Tiger	Pg # 70
6	Black Lotus	Pg # 83
7	Bonnie Baroness	Pg # 91
8	Strawberry Preserve	Pg # 101
9	Guam	Pg # 129
10	Mermaids	Pg # 161
11	Hoofstock	Pg # 171
12	No Touchy	Pg # 185
13	Holy Trin	Pg # 197

TABLE OF CONTENTS

14 Unexpected Company Pg # 213

15 Cadre Pg # 223

16 Caribou Coffee Pg # 240

17 Experimental Pg # 243

18 Abandon Camp Pg # 255

19 Dirty Magazine Pg # 263

20 Stratagem Pg # 277

21 Penthouse Pg # 285

22 Steak Tartare Pg # 295

23 Exodus Pg # 309

24 Modest Measure Pg # 315

25 The Schizophrenic & The Heretic Pg # 329

26 Confession Pg # 339

TABLE OF CONTENTS

27	Vanguard	Pg # 355
28	Alexander	Pg # 361
29	Nomads	Pg # 375
30	Dru	Pg # 385
31	The Docs	Pg # 399
32	Banda Arc	Pg # 415
33	Bird's Eye View	Pg # 439
34	Elysium	Pg # 451
	Author Biography	Pg # 471

CHAPTER ONE

Beginning of the End

A HEAVY-BODIED MOON hung on the horizon, obscured intermittently by clouds playfully teasing the watchman. Appearing later with summer constellations twinkling brightly above, underneath nestled the earth, sea, and a sleepy vessel bobbing 100 miles off the coast. Tinges of light emerged from the east, threatening dawn. The salty spray misted Phan and his crewmates, who lived as if born of the sea.

Teetering on the deck's surface, his sea legs had lost agility thanks to the bourbon on his lips. The other whalers bedded down below deck hours ago. Resigned to resume his duty after tedious wandering, he returned to the crow's nest to watch for the Philippine Coast Guard. This entity could bring its illegal operation to an abrupt and unpleasant end. As he reached the top rung and mounted the platform, he stilled. He spotted what appeared to be an impossibly gargantuan fin through his drunken stupor.

Only half believing his eyes, he barked for the captain as he half-climbed, half-slipped down the ladder, making way for his fearless leader to reach the perch. The captain wasted no time responding to the panic in the young sailor's voice.

"Are they near?" the captain barked in Tagalog, peering through the darkness from the unlit craft. Fearful of the worst, he assumed that he'd been beckoned by the policemen of the sea. Unable to decipher the sailor's babbling above the howl of the wind, he gave up. Squinting through the darkness, he searched for the lights of an approaching vessel. When he failed to see any, he diverted his attention back to Phan, suddenly feeling foolish.

Too many times, he'd seen men experience imagined fear induced by a cocktail of sleep deprivation, exhaustion, and alcohol. It was not an easy life they led, but the substantial sum from a harvest of rare bounty was worth the risk of poaching the entire season. With his nervous tension ebbing, he couldn't help but chuckle, warming with the feeling of having dodged a bullet. He felt as if their operation was nearly taken down, but then… wasn't! Amused, he descended the ladder of his tiny observation deck when the familiar sound of a breach in the water pricked his ears.

"Phan! Look Alive!" he commanded in delight. Never had a whale breach so near the ship. The loud sound of falling water boded well. This one would fetch him an excellent purse. Having retaken his position up top, he skimmed the darkness seeking his target. He squinted into the night when he noted his man's failure to follow orders and spotted him crumpled up, holding onto the rail.

"Little Phan? Are you sick, boy?" he heckled from his throne.

"Creature!" Phan shrieked in reply.

The captain's stomach clenched. Phan's voice, thick with terror, didn't portray the ramblings of a drunk but the real fear of a seasoned sailor who knew actual danger. The captain's grin vanished.

Scanning the water more carefully, he stepped down from his post, returning to the helm to relight the ship. Ablaze, he hurried back out onto the deck, calling out to the rest of his crew. His blood turned to ice as he struggled to give orders for his men to gather. They all hurried to the poop deck, a well-rehearsed group like clockwork. They grabbed their hats and jackets and came out from below, ready until they saw the beast that loomed just feet from the *End of Days*, casting a dark shadow as the sun rose over the horizon.

"Ready the harpoon!" the captain squawked. The men broke loose from shock and into action. Amazingly, like a colony of ants, they worked in unison to crane the heavy equipment, pulling levies and taking aim. Releasing, the spear whooshed, unswerving, at its target. The company fell silent, waiting, the rope whirring past, crank turning as the ship's death dagger flew interminably. Their harpoon struck the animal's hide. They all stood in anticipation and watched in disbelief as it failed to penetrate her hide and fell away.

Unfazed, the beast sank, leaving a trail of bubbles, their craft bobbing dangerously. The crew stood motionless, stunned and unsure of what was to come.

Silently, they stood, every hair standing on end. Each nerve prickled, as if waiting for a bullet to exit the smoking barrel of a gun aimed at them.

They looked at each other as if to ask, *Did that just happen?* A few found the courage to peek into the water, seeing nothing. Phan was alert, eyes darting between his brothers in arms and his captain… questioning what that animal might have been.

Without warning, a collision knocked them to the deck—everyone except Phan, who starfished the railing. The behemoth surfaced, causing a massive wave breaching.

A chorus of screams rang out. Tear-streaked faces recited prayers in hopes of salvation as the craft was lifted high. They repented, tearfully whispering hurried goodbyes.

The youngest ran seeking cover below deck. Holding his breath, he peeked out the porthole.

Darkness.

He moved closer, fogging the window with panicked breath.

As the fog cleared, his eyes focused, and he saw the ribbing of a throat. The beast drifted backward.

Teeth. She had several rows of serrated blades that seemed intelligently designed for grabbing, ripping, and tearing. Flexing her muscles, her jaw protruded beyond her broad snout in a horrifying display. She presented rows of gyrating scythes, sawing in opposing motions.

As she repelled further back, he noticed the pulsing of her monstrous gills moving her fins systematically. The beast moved, maneuvering herself delicately. Looking intently into the vessel, her large, catlike eye narrowed: searching. It was so fascinating he forgot to be afraid, secure within the ship's safety. The tapetum lucidum of her mirror-like pupil flashed reflectively through the cabin.

Ducking to dodge the searching flash of her eyeball, his heart throbbed, his eyes squeezed so tight he saw spots. Back to the wall, he told himself to calm down. In and out, he panted, his heart racing, one hand covering his eyes and the other clutching his chest. Sweat dripped from his brow. Blinking, he noticed the childish feeling of soiling his pants, warm and sticky, pressing smoothly between his flesh and underwear.

In a subaqueous explosion, his lungs were filled with water as she drove through the hold of the frigate, entering the cabin. Before he could react, his torso was severed cleanly from his trunk. Satisfied with the man held delicately within her jaws. She gave one vigorous flip of her keel, splintering the boat.

The men on the deck were flung into the air. Remains of the vessel tipped toward the horizon. Airborne, in slow motion, the men could see their foe in full view and gazed upon her prehistoric magnificence. Within a moment, the water turned crimson. Torn asunder were those who had made their fortune by turning the Asiatic waters red with the lifeblood of gentle whales.

Their screams, drowned by tidal waves of powerful jaws, finding them individually with dead-gray eyes, hunting remorselessly. Their boat was a battered toy. This monstrosity and the vengeful sea worked in harmony. In a moment, they were done. One disembodied arm remained clinging to a piece of the hull.

Task concluded, the infinydon swam on, creating a mile-long wake with her powerful tail, poaching weapons disabled, appetite unabated by her meal. She headed south, seeking. The only evidence of her encounter with this ill-fated crew was the blood-soaked harpoon, which hung still attached to a piece of floating wreckage.

CHAPTER TWO

Dominion

~ 30 Days Earlier ~

THE EGYPTIAN COTTON of his hotel creased as he sat up, sleep interrupted by his phone. It hummed, signaling the CEO of Dominion Petroleum. The digital tune of Gran Vals rang out at 2:47, alerting Quality Control, Safety, and Environmental Manager Alexander Becker that this was not a call to ignore. Never mind the miraculous quality of REM that he had been experiencing. A frantic voice buzzed on the other end of the line, confirming this was serious.

"How bad?" Alex asked Tawny Townsend, rubbing sleep from his eyes. Stretching, involuntarily flexing his bicep, he caught sight of himself in the gold-plated mirror on the far side of the room in the New York high-rise. Pensively rubbing his stubble, the faint light from his phone illuminated his chiseled features. This suite was his residence for the week while brokering business out east. He responded mechanically, tuning back into the conversation, waking more fully.

"Of course." He paused, listening. "Yes. I'll compose a preliminary press release," he stretched, as she gave a directive. "Yes. Wheels up in two hours? On my way." He ended the call and put his head in his hands, briefly regrouping in an attempt to digest the gravity of the devastation:

His mind absorbed the facts: 300 dead, the rig a total loss; billions of dollars gone. *How in the hell could this happen?* he wondered. Naked, he entered the bathroom to shave and shower. He washed quickly, hot water hitting his sculpted back and shoulders. Standing in front of the mirror, he groomed himself, dressed only from the waist down. He mulled, devising a politically acceptable explanation for the press.

He entered the chilly New York air and quickly spotted the inky black car sent for him. It glided forward as he approached the curb. The Mercedes engine purred politely as he opened the door and instructed, "JFK."

"Yes, Sir." The driver pulled off, melting soundlessly into the burgeoning traffic. Alex pulled out his phone to make a call and then put it down.

"Good morning, Frederick," smiling wryly at his driver. It was unlike him to be so curt, let alone to such good help.

"Good morning to you, Sir," the driver said, tipping his hat, making eye contact through the rear-view mirror briefly before his eyes darted back to the traffic. He tapped the brakes to avoid hitting the vehicle that seized that split second of hesitation to dart out in front. "I thought you were in New York until Friday, but it's no matter. To the airport, we go." The driver chatted warmly, continually thankful to work with such a gracious and generous client. Alex patted the driver's shoulder in thanks, nodded in apology, slid a philanthropic tip into the driver's hand, and then, pulling out his phone, made a video call.

"Townsend? Becker here. I am on my way," he reported, keeping mental notes of the numbers. He listened carefully as Ms. Townsend, the young, capable, surprisingly inexperienced CEO of Dominion Petroleum, rattled off the information she'd just learned, followed by well-thought-out directives. He observed her composure during the video chat. She always impressed him. She also had very nice, full lips. But it was her azure eyes that gripped him. He wondered about her race, noting the exotic slant of her eyes framed by well-groomed eyebrows. Studying her freshly coiffed hair, he realized he was a little smitten with her. His thoughts wandered, curious about how she looked without makeup, with her hair tumbling loose around her shoulders.

“It’s the Mariana rig,” she barked, a thinly veiled bite, conveying unappreciation for his lack of attention.

“I know, it’s bad,” he admitted. "That many?” He hung his head. "I will," he said, nodding. "Headed there now. I’ll be in the air within the hour. I’ll keep you posted.”

He ended the call, thinking, *How could this have happened?* The geological survey revealed it was a safe dig site for the greatest cache of oil in decades. This reserve was supposed to catapult them to the top. Of course, not at the cost of lives, but those surveys determined that drilling there was safe. Well, relatively. The pressure of this explosion was so intense that nothing remained of the structure. Not a soul had survived. He thought this devastation would be like none he'd ever seen, trying to prepare himself.

"Sir," the driver interrupted. "We're nearing your destination. Five minutes."

"Thank you," Alex replied gratefully, readying his bags and himself for the next leg of his expedition.

CHAPTER THREE

The Professor

DR. EVELYN HUMBOLDT was a petite spitfire. She'd earned her doctorate against many odds. Although currently experiencing personal tumult, she was more fascinated and excited by her research subjects than ever before. Her thesis was an in-depth study of the evolution and adaptation of the order Semaeostomae and the family Ulmaridae, with a specific focus on jellyfish. She was employed at California State University as a professor and researcher, working solo for the first time in her life.

When a sophomore in college, she met a bold, beautiful, green-eyed rogue who was funny, had a remarkable intellect, and a vivid imagination. He always kept her smiling with his sense of wonder, and once she got to know him, she desired nothing more than to be a part of his incredible world. Before they began graduate school, she became Mrs. Humboldt and Doctor a few years later.

Since then, the two had worked side by side on projects mostly led by him until last spring, when tension in their marriage reached a breaking point. One night, they made the disastrous mistake of going to bed angry, and as the conflict escalated over the following week, he renounced science and decided to leave their joint department.

Within a few days, he rented an apartment in the city to escape the chaos. He searched for peace: a place where he could write in solitude and explore his interest in theology without criticism. As an accomplished double major in science and religion and one of the most charismatic professors on campus, the university was more than willing to support his interest in switching fields. With his new home closer to the school, he quickly became involved in new collaborations and research with colleagues, becoming distracted. She burned with jealousy and rage, unable to openly share her true feelings about his foolish behavior.

Their marriage was a fiery union of brilliant minds and amorous bodies. Sadly, fires that burn the brightest often don't burn eternal. Two decades later, they'd had a good run. Their harmonious relationship had become obstinate. These days, they could no longer agree.

Even though they lived separately and weren't in contact, they shared custody of a two-year-old malamute named Kanik. Every Sunday, they exchanged the dog. Each secretly looked forward to these meetings, still deeply in love but also stubborn.

She was now genuinely confused about where things had gone wrong. The cause was evident to onlookers, yet it was complicated and unclear to her.

It wasn't just one thing. Evelyn, overcome

with shame and anger from the past, couldn't imagine how he could still love her despite her many flaws. In the end, she worried that he might be better off with a new woman in his life.

On his side, burdened by guilt over his mistakes, he was living in denial. The truth was, he could no longer see her love, blinded by his own pain. He feared holding onto hope might be pointless, but couldn't let her go. The thought of life without her seemed abysmal. She was his world.

For these reasons, they each stubbornly waited for the other. Quietly, each waiting for their partner to submit: crack, express hope, or take any step so this terrible break could end, and they could safely fall into each other's arms. Every weekend for the past few months, she'd acted coldly, and he had just been a jerk—both too proud and afraid to admit their feelings about their hope of reuniting honestly.

This Friday afternoon, Evelyn was on autopilot in the lab, consumed by her anxiety about their upcoming visit. She was considering cutting her lengthy hair, her crowning jewel, the next day to see if he might notice.

If he did, would he say anything? Would he like it? Would he hate it? she wondered. She couldn't imagine that he would say anything, regardless of how it looked. Her pulse started to quicken as this internal dialogue grew louder in her mind. Shaking her head at the absurdity, she pushed the hypothetical dilemma out of her mind, laughing aloud at herself for getting offended over something that hadn't even happened.

Anyway, she enjoyed having her hair hip-length. No point in cutting it now. If he didn't want her, changing her hair wouldn't make a difference.

She told herself to stop obsessing over him and focus on these incredible little treasures. Shifting her thoughts to her new research subjects: "immortal jellyfish," as the media called them. Turritopsis dohrnii, their scientific name, was what she referred to them as. The doctor wondered how these extraordinary creatures had remained undiscovered for so long. Then again, the ocean is vast, and there is still much to be discovered.

She was deep in contemplation when someone buzzed to be let in through the lab's glass doors. She met them with a goofy grin and snickered. Hank was here! A tall, lanky, well-muscled student whose body and mind were maturing into manhood handsomely. She expected that by thirty, he'd be a beautiful mess that any partner would be lucky to catch. He was a bright but somewhat melancholy science major with exceptional musical talent. Admirably, he was willing to work and worked hard, which the doc appreciated. She greeted him warmly and told him to glove up to take some fecal samples from the nursery tanks.

"Shit! My favorite!" he responded with fictitious morose, pulling his glossy hair up into a knot. Surprised by his attitude, she turned around to see him grinning at her.

"Yes, Dear. I knew it was, so I saved the task all for you! Come on, though. You have to admit that these are some pretty fascinating feces!" With a playful expression, she did a spin and a funny tap dance, trying to sell him on her perspective . She ended the number with the tip of an imaginary top hat and some dazzling jazz hands.

"Yep!" he said in good-humored defeat, raising his eyebrows at her and snapping the gloves on his wrists like always.

She was cute, he thought warmly. He admired her, and she never gave him the real shit work like mopping. Working here was good for him. With a disarming smile, he examined each specimen with focus and proficiency, recording his findings as he worked. She watched him nodding to the rhythm of whatever caterwauling was being birthed out of the end of his earbuds, one implanted in his ear canal, the other dangling so he could still listen if need be.

Evelyn finished her inventory and followed behind her assistant, gathering the dirty slides and beakers that needed washing. She bypassed the step of placing them on a tray. It was just a few items, and she turned to head to the sink. Struck by the urge to ask him if he'd seen the hilarious picture she'd hung of him on the bulletin board in the common area, knowing this would make him cringe, she turned. The toe of her shoe caught on the centrifuge cord, and she fell, glass shattering all around. The wind was knocked out of her, and she rolled onto her back, gasping, when she noticed a rather deep gash on her palm and tried to sit up.

"Jeez! What the hell?" was Hank's way of asking what happened. He knelt over her and the broken glass, quickly becoming an impressively bloody mess. "Easy, Doc. Just hold on a sec," he coddled.

"Oh! That cord is *what*!" she fussed, realizing she was to blame, knowing all loose cords should be taped to the floor. She shooed him away. "I'm fine," she promised. Despite her protest, he helped her up and hovered as she walked carefully to the sink, leaving a bloody trail. Putting her hand under running water, Hank saw that, though deep, it was a relatively small cut; it would probably be more helpful for him to clean up the mess than to pester. Grumbling, she held her hand under the running water and spotted a tiny shard sticking out. She grabbed a pair of tweezers and yanked, lecturing him on safety precautions in a lab, explaining that this could have been worse. She'd seen a nasty lab accident, she preached.

"Even though these rules seem nitpicky, they've been written for good reason. Scientists don't make pointless rules. They need to be followed if you plan to work in a laboratory. It's black and white: uncomplicated," she trailed off, now more to herself than to him, wincing as she squeezed the cut, examining the wound for further debris. Quieting, she peered into the open laceration, closely assessing the damage. She decided butterfly bandages would fix this, not wanting her mistake to become university business with an accident report and gossip.

"Yep," he said, filling up the mop bucket. Pulling out the other earbud just in case she said something important. “Should really follow the rules, Doc,” he agreed. “You sure you’re okay?” When she didn’t answer, he said to himself, “I like this song,” and reinserted one bud.

Then to her… or himself, he said, “Hey, I like this song by ‘Pianos Become the Teeth.’ I think I want to get that tattooed on me, maybe on my butt, with a yellow flower or something. That would be gangster. Probably the right cheek, not the left,” he muttered and kept working.

“You could,” she envisioned. "Marigolds are very gangster! But how many people would see a tattoo on your rear end?” she asked, quizzically amused.

"Lots of people!" he proclaimed with conviction. "I'm in a band!" he reiterated to clarify. They laughed.

Feeling a little woozy, she was thankful he was here. Her assistant brought the first aid kit and a stool. He put the cleaning supplies away and sat next to her, watching as she disinfected and wrapped her hand. Observing her, he shared his plans for the weekend.

"Saturday, my band has a gig in Long Beach. That venue has the best fish tacos. I've never played there, but I went before when my boy Marco played there. We said I was his boyfriend, and they let me in for free." His eyes beamed with the sweet memories of him and friends out on the town. "Instead of money, they paid in tacos, which were so worth it. I ate fifteen tacos because he hates fish, and they were just there. Plus, my ex had just broken up with her man. So, you know. You never know!" he smiled, shrugging.

"You lost me!" she proclaimed.

"Her best friend told my little brother that she was thinking of seeing me there. So, I mean.... You know!" he explained eloquently.

"Okay. Yes. I think I know," she chuckled, almost envying his carefree youth. Then again, not. Although the young man had a world of glittering, unknown possibilities before him, he had an uphill climb ahead to find himself. Her bright future all figured out; she just needed to seize it. She had everything she wanted except for one thing.

Hmmm.... If only Adem would make a move,

she daydreamed. One of the things she admired about her husband was his adamant nature. As Evelyn and Hank followed the procedure to close the lab for the week, she leaned over the giant aquarium to admire her precious specimens, Hank crouching down to get a side view.

"Look at that one," she puzzled. "It's grown significantly in just a day or two."

"Which one?" he asked.

"That one. The bigger one!" she said, pointing from above. A fat droplet of blood rolled from her palm, down her fingertip, and into the water.

The animal touching the droplet morphed, displaying six serpentine appendages with jaws. Violently, it breached the water's surface. As the crimson stimulus dissipated, they observed the creature revert to aimless shapes. They turned and locked eyes.

“What the fuck?” Hank spoke first. "What *was* that?” he raved. Not having an answer or point of scientific reference, she sat at a loss for words!

“Do it again!” he exclaimed excitedly.

“Yes,” she acknowledged logically. He pulled out his phone and removed both earbuds, indicating she had his full attention. There is no higher-level display from Hank than no earbuds.

“I’m recording! Go!” he prompted.

She moved to touch her thumb to her pinky, causing another droplet to travel down her palm, her middle finger, and then roll down,

down, down. She suddenly closed her fist, stopping the flow.

"No," she hesitated. "This isn't a proper setting for advanced experimentation. I mean, first, we need to collect preliminary data. We need a control group. We must establish a baseline first, or our findings may not be legitimate. I mean, they could be argued. They could be disproved. They may not even be reproducible." At this, Hank stood, placed his hands on her shoulders, leaned in so they were face-to-face, and instructed her.

"We have two tanks. One psycho fish; one regular. There's your control group and your experimental group. Do it."

"They're not fish," she mumbled, considering his reasoning and finding it somewhat sound. "Yes!" she agreed overall. "Get me the stool! I'm scared! What if it bites me?" They talked excitedly as he retrieved a step stool. She climbed the two rungs with his hand steadying her. "Ready?" she asked, prompting him to record.

He nodded, standing back, feet splayed, preparing to take the video of a lifetime. She looked at him.

"No," she shook her head with resolve.

"Yes!" he determined.

"Okay," she agreed. She looked, confirming he was ready.

"Go," he directed impatiently.

She squeezed her hand. They watched breathlessly as the rotund droplet of blood rolled and hit the water. Bewildered, they both sat watching nothing out of the ordinary. The animals undulated and swam about harmlessly as usual.

"Do it right on top of them. Aim for the big one again," he suggested, still filming. Nonplussed, she began to follow his instructions. She turned her torso to position her hand over the biggest, no, the smallest one, she decided out of great curiosity. She paused.

"Are you sure we should?"

"DO IT!" he cut her off. She squeezed her hand, and two droplets fell, making the three closest specimens lurch and morph, nearly cannibalizing each other until the blood dissipated. Then quickly reassumed a gelatinous form that floated, as gently as lilies on the water. The scientist looked at her young apprentice, astonished. He was now recording her and her face.

"Doc?" he asked as she stared blankly. "Did we just invent something?"

"Invent? No, but discover? Yes! Something HUGE! Holy moly! Holy moly!" She exclaimed, hurriedly climbing down from the stool with one hand. Stealing her from the last step, picking her up, he hugged her excitedly. They danced around and talked enthusiastically until they saw four people outside the testing center looking in curiously.

"Shhh...." she chuckled. "Settle down. This is big! The research will be taken away from me and given to someone higher up on the food chain if this isn't handled with kid gloves; this project is mine. Hank! This is important. Don't tell anyone. Don't share that video with anybody! Except me! Send that to me immediately!"

"Got it! No one! I mean, I already posted it to Snap, but I only have like 25 friends on there, and they're all dumb. Well, kind of dumb. I mean," he searched, "They don't look at my streaks anyway! It's no big deal," he assured her confidently. She stared at him, dumbfounded. "Yeah. Okay. I'll take it down."

"Thank you. So, what do I do now? I can't trust this with anyone. Who do I talk to? This is groundbreaking!"

"Dr. A.," he replied densely, as in Dr. Adem Humboldt, which Hank had grown used to calling him since there were previously two

Dr. Humboldts in the lab.

What? My Adem? Oh, no. I can't. Besides, he's no longer a scientist.

"Ummm… "I know you're all lovesick and all that, but you can. Also, he's, like, the smartest guy in the universe except you, and he is still a scientist even if he's making out with the Bible right now. He cares about this stuff and you, and then… maybe you two can-" Raising his eyebrows up and down in unison. "Huh?" he smiled. Perplexed, she glanced down at his hands and saw him perform some libidinous finger actions between his right and left hands.

She slapped his hands down, grimacing. "Weirdo!" she responded, laughing despite being embarrassed.

"Just call him," he said, sighing as he unlocked his phone and read a message from his TikTok account. "Well, my ride's here. Yeah, are you sure you're okay? I've gotta go."

"Yes. I'm fine! Thank you very much, young scholar," she said, smiling, overwhelmed by her affection for him. "Goodnight," she said, shooing him away.

He slung his bag over his shoulder, letting himself out. She headed toward her office to sit in preponderance. She turned back when she heard the door slide closed. "Good work today," she hollered after him.

He waved without looking back, as casually as any other day, both earbuds in, probably listening to 'Children with Teeth' or whatever. After locking the door, she was overcome with the feeling that she was holding a priceless treasure that needed careful protection. She shut her office door, turned off the light, and sank into her chair as she often did when alone. Her marine aquarium cast a verdant glow over the office. Relaxing, she listened to the bubbling water.

Alone, she reflected on what she had just witnessed, questioning her perception. Refocusing, she saw a striking resemblance to images on the dust jacket of her old mythology and political science books on her long-neglected bookshelf. Her expression lit up with exhilaration, confusion, and disbelief. She picked up the hardcover of **Leviathan or The Matter, Forme and Power of a Common-Wealth Ecclesiastical and Civil**, written by Thomas Hobbes and published in 1651. Hers was an authentic print from 1909. According to the prologue, the depicted beast was described as a creature washed ashore after a typhoon. Looking at that ancient image, she experienced an incredible epiphany.

CHAPTER FOUR

Specter

DELSIN BUCK woke with a start, dark eyes blinking as he was jolted awake by the screeching brakes of the morning train. From his camp near the tracks, he felt more connected to nature than in any of the dark passageways he'd slept in over the past year. The young man considered his gray tent, sheltered by these proud trees, a decent makeshift home—at least for now. Living in Broken Arrow, Oklahoma, near the tracks wasn't ideal, but he enjoyed the elder groves of cypress, dogwood, and elm. The grove provided shade from the sun and shelter from the night winds. It was peaceful. He could hear birds in the morning and smell the rushing water from Arcadia Lake. This spot was lacking one thing: nourishment.

Kicking his way free of his Coleman Autumn Trails sleeping bag, he was damp with sweat. This blessed sack had saved him last winter, but had since become a sweatbox with the arrival of spring. He wondered why he didn't just sleep on top of the bag, cushioned from the rocky ground, but found he liked the security of being wrapped up tight. Wrestling the tongue out of his right boot, pulling the leather on without bothering to untie the laces, stood ready.

A wise man would stay in the city where resources abound, his internal monologue badgered, *but first food and drink,* his mind reasoned. *Definitely drink,* he thought. Every day, he woke up parched, eyes bloodshot from the previous day's drinking. He picked up a mostly empty water bottle and grimaced as the tepid, stale fluid failed to quench his thirst. While the liquid eased the tightness of his desiccated throat, it wasn't enough. Vodka is his drink of choice, his medicine, to quiet the many voices in his head.

Delsin was a twenty-one-year-old Cree native. He was considered a *kithla,* or someone who *knows things,* in the community where he was raised. The Cherokee tribe viewed these individuals as prophets who could communicate with the Great Spirit. Unfortunately, the Great Spirit was not very pleased with his people or the Earth's current inhabitants. The actions of humankind and the current state of our world were seen as a cacophony of sins.

Many days, Delsin peddled glimpses of his visions for cash at the intersection of Kenosha and First. He used to repress them and try to keep his revelations to himself, but in the last year or so, they'd begun to roar, and the only way he could keep his sanity was to express them to anyone who would listen. Del had always been hardworking. He'd worked at the store on the res for many years, which kept his mom and sister fed. Recently, the spirits seemed to have taken up permanent residence in his head. He could no longer work or live his life among his people.

Shamefaced, he hit the road, drinking heavily to drown out the noise. Earlier this year, he was institutionalized after being found in a bad state in Oklahoma City. When police tackled and arrested him, he was covered in self-inflicted wounds. The hospitalization helped him find relief. The drugs there created a soothing mental fog and blackout that surpassed alcohol.

During his 48-hour intake, the on-call physician diagnosed Del with Schizoid Personality Disorder and heavily sedated him due to his severe episodes. Unfortunately, the physician who started on Monday discharged him, believing him a drug seeker, hastily, without any aftercare. Since then, he's been chasing that bliss only the specter named Risperidone could deliver.

Having rinsed off the night's sweat at his small water reservoir, he donned a flannel over his yellowing undershirt. The clothing did little to hide his thick build, ragged jeans snugly fit his sturdy frame, and size thirteen boots with frayed laces slapped the ground.

Dressed and somewhat washed, he journeyed to his usual spot. He carried a dingy coffee can labeled "Change for Change" in white acrylic. As the voices began to chatter, he pursed his lips and shook his head, begging for peace as his almond eyes stared into emptiness, grappling with dark prophecies of the end.

Stationed at his post, he sat cross-legged, leaned back into the stop sign, and permitted the fog of the ancestral guides to fill his mind. When the clouds began to settle, he began to vocalize what came to the forefront of his consciousness.

"Hi-ye-gi! Wake up, my brothers and sisters. Our world," he paused, seeming to be observing something in another realm, "She is crying! When white invaders first came to our land, ambassadors of the Great Spirit were sent to guide them through the land and beg for peace in the countryside. 'You may harvest, but you must not rape. You may hunt, but do not murder,' they were told. Like my warrior ancestor, Kennekuk of the Kickapoo tribe said, 'My father, the Great Spirit, has placed us all on this earth; he has given our nation a piece of land. Why do you want to take it away and give us so much trouble?' He learned through death and resurrection that, regardless of race or religion, peace and prayer, guided by the divine, are the only ways to live. Use your Christian church altar and your One True God, or ancient prayer sticks, to seek truth. We must preserve our paradise, our earth, or damnation will soon come. Repent and show temperance, for she is coming. I see her approaching our shores. My elders have often foretold crises in the past: Smallpox, the Long Walk, and now a new virus. We must stand and renounce our greed and do the Ghost Dance again. We must call on the favor of our spirit guides and grieve now for the pretty princess. She and her people have been lost and can never be recovered. She will not fall alone, my brothers and sisters. We shall all turn to ash together!"

His wailing faded, visions fading, while he regained consciousness. Suddenly self-aware and embarrassed, his throat constricted, anxious tears streaming down his cheeks. He collapsed from a stiff sitting position onto his elbows on the sidewalk. Blinking, he wiped his face with a dirty sleeve.

Looking down, he saw his coffee can filled with a five-dollar bill, several ones, and change. A cold cup of coffee sat at his feet, left behind by a kind passerby. Breathing raggedly, slowing his heart rate, unfolded himself from his trance-like position. He noticed a boy recording him from the balcony of a third-floor apartment. Caught, the kid ducked back into the window, snickering. Immediately, the kid uploaded the video to Donut Diggler Kid's YouTube account, where his 114 subscribers eagerly awaited some fresh hilarity. Diggler Kid uploaded it without editing and then browsed YouTube for any new clips posted since he logged off an hour earlier.

As he scrolled through videos, he passed a Dateline story about the mysterious disappearance of the Bonnie Baroness's cruise liner. He ended up watching clips of footballers and gym rats passing gas at the worst moments.

Delsin was rigid from sitting on the pavement. He lost track of time in those states. Slowly, he rose, stretching. The shadows on the sidewalk said it was midday. He picked up the small cup of coffee and drank it in a few gulps: stagnant, cold, and bitter. He shivered and gave thanks for the offering. He envisioned it was left by a woman with a small dog, afraid but hopeful for the man on the street. It could have been anyone. That was more of a notion than a prophetic vision like those that overtook him.

Feeling encouraged by these tokens, he decided to get a bite to eat and a pint of Imperial vodka. That should hit just hard enough to let him fall asleep without a hangover. Clarity was necessary for the following day when he had his visions. He just needed temporary respite from the clamor, not total silence. He had a sense that his attention to his visions was more critical than ever. Time was of the essence.

CHAPTER FIVE

Tasmanian Tigers

DOCTOR EMMIE LONGORIA heard a rumor, a delicious rumor, that on the mainland of Australia, there were sightings of Tasmanian Tigers: Thylacinus cynocephalus. There have been over 7000 documented sightings. An animal that the scientific community has deemed to have gone extinct nearly 100 years ago. Previously abundant, this animal was hunted mercilessly. Furthermore, their well-being was jeopardized due to habitat loss resulting from human encroachment. Once the countryside became an agricultural region and thylacine fed on livestock for survival, farmers went on a mission to eradicate them. In the 1930s, the animal believed to be the last was captured and housed as a captive until its death.

Emmie was pursuing an extension of her Ph.D. studies as a media research journalist, with a minor focus on the biological studies of obscure and extinct species. This distinguished young lady was investigating the existence of a thylacine doe who'd been reported with a pair of joeys. There was a river basin where the trio had been caught on trail cams by the Department of Primary Industries, Water and Environment. Emmie believed they were living in the area. She needed definitive proof to put them back on the CITES list, the Convention on International Trade in Endangered Species of Wild Fauna and Flora, to ensure their protection.

She was granted a review of the footage of misidentified "dingos" gnawing on the head of a kangaroo carcass at night. Seeing the animals hop and pounce in a way that was not mechanically canine, spotting their short ears, elongated, alligator-like jaws, slender bodies ending in thick tails, all told her these were a female thylacine with her young. Only after she digitally brightened the footage could she see a faint outline of seventeen telltale tiger stripes on the doe.

This footage prompted her trip to the outback, where she planned to camp out with her Nikon D850 DSLR Camera. Abandoning her Subaru at her campsite, she lugged her drape, a mat, snack pack, and a tripod downhill. She intended to set up a fort in a thicket, staying up all night for several weeks, photographing the nocturnal wildlife until she caught sight of her target. Slapping at the insect threatening to sting her right shoulder, she spied the perfect copse of trees near the river, yet uphill enough to give her a clear vantage, and quietly put out her gear. Beaming at the complex chorus of the night announcing the setting sun: calls of wedgebills and their kin warbling, wild cockatoos crying, amphibians crooning, all harmonizing with the sounds of mammals who'd slept through the heat now beginning to rouse.

Camp set up, she settled into a comfortable position, watching the rushing water through a large peephole in her bivouac. Silently, she unhitched her canteen from the thong on her backpack. Cautiously, she took a few cool, deep pulls from the metallic portal, comforted by the titanium aftertaste that lingered as she drank from this trusty old vessel. This bottle belonged to her father, who carried it with him during his overseas travels. He was a tough man, brutish, but a brilliant, gentle giant. Drinking from this flask felt as close to a hug from her father's strong arms as she could get while alone in the bush. This man pushed her to chase her dreams no matter the cost. She finally reached her dream destination through blood, sweat, and hardship. Now graduated, her studies were funded by the Wonambi Conservatory Coalition, a group of wealthy preservationists who hire researchers and zoologists to study wildlife, especially endangered Australian species and a few recently classified extinct ones. With all her travel costs covered and a generous weekly stipend, she could focus on her work—free from the troubles that plagued her during graduate research.

With the number of evening rays casting a carmine hue over the landscape, the cicadas started their song of the bush, announcing the warm evening as summer nightfall arrived. Lying back on her pack roll, knowing she would hear rustling if larger animals approached, she listened. She gazed at the twinkling stars that winked at her from the sky. Breathing deeply, she inhaled the scent of eucalypts and river water. She heard a rustling at the edge of her blind. Alert, she sat up, knowing she might encounter venom. She was pleased when a common legless lizard, the scaly-footed creature, slithered over her bag and out of the other side of her hide, paying her no attention. Pygopus lepidopodus, she mused. Did you evolve from, or are you evolving into, a serpent? she wondered. She was pulled from her thoughts when she heard the drumming wingbeats of some sparrows. She peeked from her peephole to watch a flock dancing and playing on the rocks at the water's edge, dipping their toes and beaks in, chirping a merry tune. They were quickly joined by a starling mimicking their song, which soon began its own lively whistling tune: Sturnus vulgaris, Emmie identified. Grabbing her audio recorder, she captured the sounds. As the tape rolled, she adjusted the knobs to catch the amusing call of a distant Kookaburra.

Now that dusk had fallen, she began to observe through her camera lens and saw thorny lizards, stag beetles, and a quiet mob of kangaroos for hours. Each from their respective camps came to drink and cool off. It wasn't until the moon traveled across the sky and became shrouded by the northern mountain range that she was overcome by fatigue. The lull of wildlife and the passivity required by a photographer in hiding led her to take a fifteen-minute nap. Setting her watch to vibrate when the small hand reached four, she settled her head on her backpack, reaching up to move her long, thick braid from underneath her. She spread her button-up flannel over her goose-pimpled arms like a throw blanket to lessen the naked feeling of sleeping outside in the outback.

She felt peacefully insignificant in the open, the stars staring down at her. *What a big, giant world this is,* she reflected. Dozing, she heard large soft feet padding as if in a trot, halting, unsure. She lay still, breath held, and squinted into the darkness as if that would sharpen her hearing. Unable to hear over the chirp-hum orchestra of Gryllotalpa's cricket song in the grass, she exhaled, ribs expanding beneath her hands. Maybe she had dreamt the experience, she considered. Letting her eyes flutter closed again, knowing her respite was nearly spent, she hearkened. Taking a deep belly breath, she smiled, realizing, whether she found what she sought or not, there was nowhere else she'd rather -

Thought cut short, she heard a yip followed by a strange growl, making her hair stand up. Her body stiffened, desperately wanting to look out. Lying still, she hit record on her camera, fearing that if she jostled, she'd spook the animals she knew were thylacines. She heard padded footsteps break the surface of the water, along with smaller bodies splashing carelessly, a mother wolf's grunt seeming to hush them. The joeys quieted and swam silently. She could hear the water sloshing as they moved in and out. Finally, she heard a scuffle, accompanied by the playful sounds of wet paws and the purring of the doe from the water. With this commotion, she sat up to spy. With clenched abs, she rose without disturbing her hide. As her pulse raced in excitement, she saw white splotches.

Upright, she closed her left eye, peering out. There was a two-and-a-half-foot-tall Tasmanian Tiger with her three joeys. Her striped back shimmered as droplets of water rolled off her coat. Gracefully, she left the water, her belly full, and gathered the kids to head home. Repressing the urge to clap her hands excitedly, she clenched her fingers and bit her knuckle. Checking the lens to ensure she was capturing them, she saw that she was aimed too far to the right and turned the rig, which made the tiniest squeak. Hearing this sound, Mother stood on her hind legs, glaring into the darkness. Wiggling her nose, she cataloged the unfamiliar scent she detected. She reviewed her database of odors and decided this one signaled danger. With authority, she stomped her hind foot, producing a surprising sound—a hissing—which brought her joeys to attention. They looked at her for guidance. She bounded away from the water, breaking into a sprint. The three joeys followed close behind. Emmie sat in awe, silent, pulse pounding in her ears. She wanted to shout it from the rooftops. Luckily, she didn't have to, as a roost of flying foxes began screeching beyond the clearing over a disagreement, while the sun started to paint the horizon pink with the promise of a new day.

CHAPTER SIX

Black Lotus

ANTON ISAAC CLOSED his browser windows, clicked to start his ritual data wipe, and shut down his Alienware laptop. Squinting, he pushed his glasses up his nose and gave a covert wave to the Black Lotus Coffee Shop staff. He shouldered his messenger bag, grabbed his keys, and turned to leave. Today, a suspicious newcomer appeared in the shop. Anton's programming detected a breach — not just any violation, but from an intruder within a twenty-foot radius. *'Government sucker!'* he thought, sending a seedy bot back to the hacker that would infect her computer and everyone on her network. He'd be halfway to Palm Springs before she caught wind of his antics, tossing her coagulated coffee in fury. He loved the game, and he played it well.

Anton didn't have a traditional job. Neurodivergent, he was a technical savant. Much to his mother's dismay, he'd amassed significant wealth by writing code for Bitcoin at the age of eleven. When his parents told him to take his bath and go to bed, Anton took that as his cue to party. He spent late nights surfing and hacking on the pink glitter Nintendo DS that his sister had thrown out. By ten, he'd been banned from using technology because he was obsessed, concerning his parents. Being on the spectrum, they sheltered him and worried about his ability to self-regulate. Flash forward one decade.

More remarkable than how he gained his fortune was how, at twelve, he'd lost over $2.3 million. It was stored on a Transformer jump drive that his blind and deaf chihuahua ate, thanks to a misplaced glob of peanut butter. On that particular day, he was late in serving her a second lunch because of a delayed school bus. When he found it some days later, he didn't bother touching it. Instead, he chose to earn his money back through the stock exchange rather than through feculence.

His family believed he paid his bills by taking on odd tech jobs found on LinkedIn and coding for small start-ups. The only legitimate position he'd held was in 2018, when he wrote a cute little algorithm for an Indian YouTube account that showcased music videos aimed at increasing its subscriber count. They found immense success directly after and continue to grow.

Anton spent time as a blogger on the dark web, specializing in viral conspiracy theories. On one occasion, he'd been approached by the FBI offering well-paid employment, which he rejected. His issue was that they wanted to cage an otherwise free bird. They were going to force him to sit in an office for forty hours a week under observation and follow their rules. He envisioned the government holding him captive between four sterile walls, wearing stiff, strangling clothes with too many buttons pinching his wrists and neck, and corduroy pants. *Give me death before you give me corduroy,* was his motto. With his sensory integration, touching the ribbed material felt was akin to electrical shock. *No, thank you.* Worst of all, they had regulations. He would have to follow their unspoken code of conduct like an alien robot. He'd be forced to walk to the water cooler for a sip of water, smiling at strangers.

The idea triggered his nervous tics. They would consider his supervision a matter of national security if they were to divulge their undercover operations to him. Amusingly, he already knew all of their secrets, and couldn't care less. What did concern him? Major injustice, the welfare of the planet, his new chihuahua, and, come the holidays, family. He always hoped to find his family safe in their farmhouse in Texas, sitting around a beautiful conifer just waiting for, relieved to see that he had stayed out of harm's way. Well, mostly. There was that one situation in 2017. However, it was never pursued. As soon as the warrant was issued for his arrest, it vanished, lost in cyberspace. Imagine that!

Putting his Jeep into gear, he pulled away from the curb and glanced in his rear-view mirror with a smug look, nodding at himself after seeing no one on his tail. After picking up speed, he noticed that his passenger tire was limping. He drove cautiously another block or two, making a few turns to find a discreet location, and pulled over. Rolling his eyes, he examined a deflating tire! *Real-world problems,* he lamented. He opened the driver's door to pop the latch and release the trunk, but suddenly, the lights went out. There was a bag over his head, arms flailing, and he was thrown off-balance by his attackers. Seconds before losing consciousness, he realized he'd finally been bested. *Bastards!* Was his fleeting thought as his body went limp. Defeated. Two gentlemen of formidable stature quickly hoisted his wiry frame into an unmarked SUV.

CHAPTER SEVEN

Bonnie Baroness

THE MARQUEZ FAMILY arrived in Galveston the night before their cruise. Boarding their ship, they planned to spend the day swimming and playing in the water park before the boat left port. The youngest of the three girls, Paulina, was the most excited, since this was her first trip to the Caribbean. She was most excited about Belize when they planned to swim with dolphins. As Thalia's eyes scanned the thousands of cabin windows, Wendy looked at the large lettering on the ship's stern. "Bonnie Baroness," she mouthed.

"What's a Baroness?" she asked her parents.

"Robert, what's a baroness?" Priscilla asked her husband, slapping him on the back, knowing herself but uncertain how to explain it exactly.

"Ow!" he said, holding his shoulder in mock pain, shifting away from his attacker, beer bottles clanking in his bag, an amused smirk lurking. "A baroness is like a queen, but less important back when they had royalty and all that. She was a baron's wife, which was a big landowner in charge of the serfs in the region."

Priscilla rolled her eyes at his accurate explanation, loving him but hating him for any advantage he had over her when it came to the worship she saw in their children's eyes. Mostly, she loved him.

The first day at sea was a glorious, indulgent event. There were mountains of food and entertainment. The views of the ocean and its creatures were mesmerizing. If you were near the edge, you could see fish and other sea life swimming below. As she lounged poolside, Priscilla watched her daughter playing on her phone. The oldest, Wendy, was stretched out on a towel, lazily eyeing the lean teenage boy across the pool. She was doing a poor job of pretending to watch funny videos through the dark lenses of her sunglasses. The younger girls were wrestling over a giant, flamingo float in the pool.

Being the rightful winner, Thalia mounted it proudly and raised her fists in a victory sign. Paulina dove underwater, crouched at the bottom, and performed an epic plunge, emerging between her sister's legs, knocking her backward, toppling her into the water. Thalia's scream of surprise was muffled as the water flooded her lungs. After mounting the flamingo she'd named Geoffrey the Pink, Paulina paddled her legs clockwise, turning her new vehicle 180 degrees to face her sister, the loser. Thalia stood in the shallow end, hair plastered over her face, rubbing the back of her head where she had been knocked. Without warning, she submerged below the water's surface and then popped up just long enough to spit out a fountain of water right into her sister's face!

"Sicko!" Paulina shrieked and started paddling after her attacker. Laughing, Thalia somersaulted backward into the water, swimming to the deep end and sitting cross-legged on the pool floor, seemingly meditating, only releasing bubbles every 30 seconds or so.

"Mother! How is she doing that?" Paulina whined. Bored after realizing she'd lost despite her victory, the youngest paddled off to the shallow end, pulling her Hello Kitty shades down over her eyes and waving farewell to all the kids without the luxury of a raft.

Priscilla slapped Robert, causing him to spill his Corona. "Are you watching this?" she asked her husband.

"Watching what?" he asked, clueless, flicking the puddle of beer out of his crotch.

"Aye, aye, aye," she chided.

"What?" he asked in profound confusion. She waved her arm in surrender.

"Never mind!" she grumbled. He raised both palms in bemusement and took another sip, enjoying the breeze. She laughed. After lunch, Wendy had wandered off and was found quietly visiting with Nic-from-Cancun on the ship's bow.

"Yeah, I totally saw you by the pool and thought you were hot," said the gray-eyed Nicolas, nervously playing with his auburn waves with his right hand.

"What? You saw me earlier? No way!" she responded in feigned surprise, slightly entertained.

"Yeah. I was gonna talk to you, but I think your mom was there, and you were on your phone. But you're hot. Are you 18?" he asked clumsily.

"Oh, my gosh!" said Wendy with her hand over her face. She looked over to see her little sisters dangerously reenacting the scene from Titanic where Rose's heart decides to go on and on. Deciding that they were more interesting than the boy, she walked away. "You guys are idiots!" she yelled, laughing as she ran over to them, abandoning the fidgety North Dakotan.

"Hey, but what's your name? I'm Nic!. I'm from Cancun!" he called after her optimistically.

"Paulina, Happy Feet, you get down from there!" Priscilla scolded, suddenly noticing all three of her girls were way too close to the edge. Smacking Robert for his lack of attention, she vacated her deck chair. Recording their antics as she rose to retrieve her children when their performance went from hilarious to dangerous.

"Look, Mama!" Paulina pointed out to the ocean, where some animals were breaking the surf.

"Dolphins!" announced Thalia delightedly, hopping up and down.

"Mija, those aren't dolphins. That's a pod of whales." Their mother corrected just as Robert walked up and put his hands on his wife's shoulders, taking in the salty sea air and the incredible view.

"What's wrong with them?" he wondered aloud. "Is that normal for them to jump out of the water like that?"

"Yes, Tonto! Haven't you ever seen videos of them doing that? I sent you that video on Facebook. You didn't even watch it, did you?" she accused.

"Which video? You send me so much," he said defensively. She raised a hand to smack him playfully, but he blocked her strike and got to the punchline first, kissing her forehead.

Suddenly, they all lost their balance as terrifying noises erupted from the water.

"I'm going to TikTok this," said Paulina. The ship shook, and the phone slipped overboard. After a loud splash, the video feed went black.

CHAPTER EIGHT

Strawberry Preserve

EVELYN DABBED RAW HONEY over toast and sipped the coffee from ground beans from the Blackbird Café off Orange Avenue, transfixed by hypnotic surf pounding the beach. Sitting atop the Redwood balcony that she and Adem had built. She teared up, smiling at the memory of them knocking over the gallon of wood stain as they made love under the stars. Scraped, exhausted, sun-kissed, and in love, they laughed as he rolled them strategically, carefully guiding her golden flesh clear of the spill without uncoupling.

However, sitting alone this morning, the breeze ruffling the edges of her hair, she was moved by bittersweet memories. Gazing pensively into the melodious sea, her slouchy knit slipped off her slender shoulder, polished toes stretched out on the hand-carved footstool.

Her night had been restless. The excitement of the event in the lab was overshadowed by her indecision. She was certain she needed to confide in a colleague, but she hadn't yet decided whom. She'd never been close with her peers, always working alongside Adem. The couple kept to themselves. Outside of her marriage, Evelyn focused on research and students rather than friendships. Though friendly and well-liked, she was indifferent to outsiders of the unbreakable domain shared with her partner. For so long, he had been her spouse, fellow researcher, and best friend. They spent their days and nights together, reveling in discovery and fulfilling their dreams. Their work hours were filled with eager teaching and in-depth lab work, while their nights and weekends were spent pursuing passions—at least until last year. The day of the incident had not been forgotten.

Her fingers traced the remnant of scars on her hands from the burns and the jagged pink reminder on her forehead. She was glad she was unconscious when it was stitched closed. The blight had grown silvery and mostly smooth now.

Eyes lowered, she acknowledged that only one researcher was suitable for this delicate task. She knew confiding in him would break their unspoken pact of silence. She hated to seem desperate, especially after revealing so much vulnerability in the past, but this was bigger than them; it was science. Pushing herself off the settee, she stepped inside to grab her phone. She looked at the analog clock standing watch in the dining room.

It's 7:30 on Saturday morning. Can't you wait until tomorrow night when he comes by to drop off Kanik? she thought. *Swallow your pride, you damned fool. We have the whole weekend ahead of us. Why waste it? Time may be of the essence here!* She battled her pride in this futile debate.

She shook her head at her dogged thinking

and clicked the contact "Beast." She hadn't had the heart to change it after he replaced his name in her phone, as hers is listed as Beauty. A private quip between them years ago. Seldom overtly romantic, he sometimes did things that nurtured her inner child. Of all people, it was he who knew her best. That was one of the many things he did that made her sure he was her better half. She typed, "Beast," and scrolled through their message log. Since the split, there had been only cordial meetings to exchange the dog. No tenderness. No concessions.

With that realization, she put the phone down, defeated. Resembling a young girl rather than a woman, she folded at the dining room table, tucked her hair behind her ear, and gnawed her bottom lip. Lost in thought, she called upon her deeply scientific brain.

Who is the best candidate for a research partner in this case? Considering experience, education, work ethic, intelligence, and trustworthiness." Squeezing her eyes closed tight, indignant but acquiescent, she had her answer.

With newfound insight, she picked up her phone, moved to dial, and then recanted. Instead, she composed the following text message: *I must see you today. Come here for brunch at 10:00 am regarding a scientific matter of great urgency.* As she always did, she proofread her message and hit send, after which she sat astonished by sudden exhilaration.

He is coming here today for a social visit. Well, not really, but she thought it was a big deal since it involved more than just a dog exchange. Excitedly, she checked her phone. *No response yet. Well, it had only been a second. My gosh!* She realized she needed a shower. *Maybe a haircut too! No! Don't start that again,* she chided herself. *Just stay cool. Don't go overboard,* she thought, squealing as she ran up the stairs to take a bath.

Knowing she had time, she took a long, hot shower to relax her stiff muscles and dressed carefully. Overjoyed, she tousled her hair and pinned it up casually. She headed to the market for fresh fruit, bread, and deli meats. When she arrived, she realized he'd not yet confirmed their appointment. Sitting in her car, her stomach clenched as she pulled her phone from her bag.

Yes, he has responded, she noted. *Of course, he had. It had been over an hour now. She opened the message. It read:*

"Can't. Have a date." Heat rose to her face,

and her eyes flooded.

"Then you can just rot in hell, you j-a-c-" she was in the process of typing when she received another message. She paused and clicked it open.

"JK. See you in 30," it read.

"Jackass!" she finished aloud before deleting the entire message. Still shaken, she composed herself, stepping out of her vehicle. Rushing through the store, she grabbed everything except grape jelly. Instead, she picked up strawberry and checked out, knowing Adem only ate grape. Driving home, her breath caught, spotting Adem lounging on the deck; Kanik wagging eagerly, waiting for his master to throw a stick from the balcony.

The man faked two hearty throws, trying to test the dog's wits, and laughed raucously when the dog flinched, looked, but didn't budge. She heard him praise the dog for his intelligence, and stood up, hurling the heavy stick an extraordinary distance; the muscles in his upper body rippled noticeably under his T-shirt. Kanik, yipping manically, clambered past her down the stairs, nearly knocking her down. His quest was to search for his new favorite toy. Struggling now between her purse, keys, and the grocery bags, she ascended the stairs, quieting her pounding heart at the sight of her husband behaving so amiably. It made her flush even though it was only toward the dog and not her. Adem came down the steps, two at a time, and, although he didn't greet her verbally, lifted the heavy canvas bags off her shoulders and walked ahead of her, unlocking the door and holding it open for her, which was classic Adem. Ignore typical convention but act like a real gentleman where it counts. She noted, hiding a smirk riddled with irritation and joyful familiarity.

She enjoyed how he took care of her when it mattered. She appreciated that he was there to lighten her load. That was what he did for her in many ways. Although he sometimes made her howl with frustration, he always looked out for her when it counted. He challenged her, too, not just like some inanimate Ken doll. He was a strong man with his own thoughts, beliefs, and opinions. It was only natural that they didn't always see eye to eye. All those thoughts raced through her mind in the five seconds it took her to climb the last few steps and duck under his bulging forearm into the kitchen.

“So… Hello! … Good morning?” she said awkwardly, flustered.

“Hi. Yeah. So, what’s up?” he quipped.

“Oh! So, no breakfast. Just straight to business?” she bristled, feeling foolish that she unwittingly expected this meeting would be more somehow.

“Well, I’ll eat. You should eat. So, yes, let’s have breakfast, but your message was… out of the blue. Are you okay?” he asked. "What happened?” he asked pointedly. He’d stopped unbagging the groceries and turned to look her square in the face.

“Well, yes," she blushed, realizing she might have been acting a bit irrationally. "It’s big!” she started, gesticulating with her hands, then crossing them on her hips defiantly, trying to regain control and keep her secret hidden, at least for a few moments. "I'm starving, for the record." He watched her, his eyes wide with interest. Noticing she was enjoying the attention from her small power play, he watched her with curiosity. "I'll need time to tell the whole story from start to finish, and I want food. I figured, why not brunch? So, let's eat," she said, sounding less eloquent than usual but remaining obtuse about the purpose of their meeting. He shrugged, never one to refuse a meal, and went back to unpacking the groceries.

"Your hand!" he brushed her arm, taking note of the fresh bandage.

"I'm fine. That's all part of it," she said. "Believe me. This was too big for just me," she admitted, half-smiling in glee at the enormity of her announcement but more by the touch of his hand and his evident expression of concern.

"All right," he relented. Having pulled out freshly baked loaves of rye and sourdough bread from the sack, his and her favorites from the corner grocery store, his stomach cramped in anticipation. He'd not eaten well living alone. He opened the fridge in search of garnish, having already spotted her local honey on the counter.

"Grape?" he asked, rummaging through the spotless, nearly empty refrigerator at a loss.

"No. I'm out. I have strawberry," she proffered, pulling the fresh jar from the bag. He turned around, knowing she did not partake in jellies, jams, or preserves, even if her life depended on it. She did not need strawberry as no one in this house ate it, especially him.

"Is this for your new boyfriend?" he asked, squaring his shoulders in mock anger.

"No. It's for you to throw at your pretty, little date," she admitted in resignation, knowing she'd been blatantly caught in a passive-aggressive act. It had seemed so much more passive than aggressive while in the store, but, in hindsight, the purchase was a petty act of vengeance.

My date was with Dr. Smith and Kanik. He has another ear infection. I was supposed to see him at 9:30, but they squeezed us in earlier when I told them you needed attention.

Peeved, "Another ear infection!" she exclaimed, trying to divert the attention away from her foolishness, flooded with relief.

"Yes. He needs a round of antibiotic drops just like before. No biggie," he responded coolly. Typical. She walked over to the big bay window and smiled, watching Kanik jump and bark at a tree, challenging a giant squirrel who was never in any real danger of being caught by him. That wily squirrel was fearless and seemed to enjoy the game, teasing the massive dog daily, chittering at him with one fuzzy paw, hurling her worst insults. Evelyn beamed at this turn of events, hugging herself, knowing that this scenario could happen again every morning if everything went as planned.

"So, I guess I'll have cereal and fruit. You?" he asked.

"Coffee," she replied. He turned away from the pantry, abandoning his search for jelly, and stared, recalling her big proclamation about her massive appetite, but then laughing, she amended, "and fruit!" I've been dying for a grapefruit!" she clarified. He rolled his eyes and sat down with his cereal, quietly waiting for her to spill the beans after a brief attempt at small talk that began with her mocking his recent professional endeavors.

"So, any new developments in the Jesus Christ Division?" He raised one eyebrow, appearing anything but charmed. He sat, chewing in silence, choosing not to engage in her banter. When her poor-humored diversion was met with a total lack of applause, she stopped deviating and explained the events of the previous day, moment by moment. He nodded now and then, encouraging her when she began the discussion earnestly and meeting her gaze when she slowed down to check in and make sure he was still listening. Finally, after each event had correctly been recounted and he'd taken a moment to digest the information, he spoke.

"Why the right cheek? And why only tattoo one side?"

"Really? That's what you are choosing to comment on?" She stood and moved closer to his side of the table. She accused him, eyes flashing with hot anger mixed with charming amusement, reminded of how funny he could be, hands outstretched as if to strangle him. His large hands gripped her wrists, and he pulled her face toward his. Now chest to chest with her hands pinned, completely defenseless, they stood still, breathing heavily. Although he was taller than she by eight inches, her lips were irresistibly close. He kissed her. Just a quick peck and then sat back down to eat again, pausing to dip his Grape Nuts into the milk and then, sincerely, asked,

"How could you sit on this all night, Evie? I was on campus. You could have picked up your office phone and dialed my extension. I could have been there in fifteen minutes!" he responded reasonably, then pulled out the chair next to him and patted it, inviting her to sit at his side. With flushed cheeks, she sat feeling warmly acknowledged. They finished their food, picking at it here and there while unraveling the scientific implications for hours: debating, reflecting, bouncing ideas and potential consequences off each other, designing theories, and deflating them as the hours slid by.

They soon discovered that it was late into the night and that they were famished. Surprised by how heavily immersed they'd become. Kanik wagged in thanks as she poured his kibble. Seeing how happy the dog was, Adem dialed their favorite place for Sushi and ordered both of their favorite dishes to be delivered so they could continue refueled and unabated.

They took turns speaking and listening, drawing sketches, and pulling books—old and new—from their library for reference. At one point in the night, she balanced, perched on top of the mantle with her hands splayed and hair flying wildly, reenacting the moment when the ravenous jellyfish devoured her blood, and he sat with a finger over his mouth, trying not to spit out popcorn. Raising a hand to speak, interrupting her epiphany as if he had reached a higher level of consciousness,

"So, this species is currently known as Turritopsis dohrnii?" he asked for confirmation.

"Yes, but that was based on the idea of them being a unique, eternal bottom feeder. Not some shape-shifting carnivore."

"Exactly. So, the species needs a new name."

Well, I would think so. Maybe Humboldtei? Usually, a species is renamed when such a significant discovery is made. I believe this justifies the creation of a new genus. Perhaps the genus should be Evelenei." She agreed, thinking aloud.

He stood abruptly, one finger raised.

Kanik slid from his lap, landing with a soft thud.

"I've got it!" he proclaimed.

"What?" she clapped. "What shall we call them?"

"It will ring simple but true," he raised one eyebrow. "Turds!"

"What? No!" She jumped up laughing and climbed him like a tree, kissing his lips, her whole body shaking with laughter. She then pulled out her Genus Turritopsis book and started listing the other species: Turritopsis is a genus of hydrozoans in the family Oceaniidae: chevalense, inquirenda, fascicularis, lata Lendenfeld." She looked up to realize she was, in fact, reading to the dog. "Hey, where'd you go?" she called.

"Peeing. I can still hear you, though. Go on!" he shouted from the bathroom.

"Well, there's minor and nutricula, pacifica, pleurostoma, polycirrha, and finally rubra. Are you sure you can hear me?" she yelled louder than before.

"Yes," he said quietly, walking back into the room. "But you didn't mention the turds." To prove that he had, in fact, heard the entire list. "And you know what's funny. At the end of their lifespan, they turn into a polyp. Do you see a theme here?" he asked her with a ridiculous grin, surreptitiously joyful at seeing his old wife again, the passionate woman he'd fallen for long ago. She grabbed his biceps and tried shaking him in exasperation. He didn't budge.

"Not turds, and now we know they do not

even turn into polyps."

"I mean, they sound like little assholes to me," he continued, not relenting, holding up her injured hand and reminding her of what she'd witnessed from the little creature just a day prior. "Imagine if you had put your finger in the water." She leapt up in excitement, pretending to beat his chest with tiny fists in exasperation, but laughed playfully. Truly unique was this woman to whom he was married, he silently mused. After this ruckus of the *turd* debacle finally wound down, the more intense dance of the intellects deepened as they discussed the implications of her discovery for hours. Eventually, the two fell asleep on the couch.

He awoke a few hours later with a kink in his neck and reluctantly got up to put on his shoes and head to the apartment, but paused. A small smile appeared on his face when he saw she had reached for him in her sleep when his warmth left the couch. His dimples flashed in surrender, and instead of putting on his sneakers, he scooped her up and carried her upstairs to bed. He removed her shoes and joggers, gently unfastening her earrings, as he knew she did when getting ready for bed. He carefully placed her clothes over the armchair and set her mother-of-pearl earrings into her jewelry box where they belonged. Shrugging out of his clothes, they dropped to the floor, and he slipped underneath the flaxen bedding next to her. Mewling, she rolled toward him, searching hands reaching out, and he wondered if she'd done this every night since he'd gone away. Knowing their separation was over, he wrapped his arms around her and pulled her into his chest. She nestled into him, purring.

The next morning, she woke in Adem's arms, where she'd only dreamt of being for months. Puzzled momentarily, her memories flooded back. She quietly covered her mouth with her hand, grinning feverishly. Needing a moment to take in the scene, she lay back down again. The whole world seemed brighter, more beautiful. Her movement gently roused him. He rolled over, his back to her. She reached with delicate hands, grazing his trapezius, scapula, and shoulder blades, fascinated by the tone and strength of his body. She withdrew, breathing deeply, enjoying the view. Grinning, she pondered this new chapter: her marriage back on track, a new scientific discovery, and... strawberry jelly that needed to be donated to whoever was willing to eat it at work. Squeezing her eyes shut, she sat up, trying to process everything. After some gentle stretches on the balcony, she rolled up her yoga mat and padded back into the bedroom quietly.

She was delighted to see him still in their bed, shirtless. She scooted back into the bed and took a moment to watch him breathe peacefully, his strong chest rising and falling. He'd kicked the blankets off while sleeping. She admired the red ink on his tawny shoulder, written there years ago in her honor. She was tempted to trace it with her finger, but chose to leave him alone.

"Totus tuus," it read. Totally yours, in Latin, to symbolize their eternal love for each other, rooted in the most scholarly language—a dead language that would live forever through their intertwined lives and studies. It mirrored the same inscription on her ribcage, her declaration of forever to him.

"My beautiful beast," she murmured. She rose, feeling renewed and relaxed despite getting only a few hours of sleep. She smiled at Kanik, who was snoring loudly as he hung off his too-small cot at the foot of their four-poster bed. She knew this was the start of a wild journey, but she'd be safe no matter what because she had the good doctor by her side, and, once again, he had her.

CHAPTER NINE

Guam

After a 20-hour nonstop flight, Alex arrived at Guam International Airport looking as fresh and presentable as he did the previous morning, despite his sleep deprivation and the sweltering humidity. It had gone from Saturday before dawn to dusk on Sunday, thanks to a long day of travel plus a fourteen-hour time difference. His first stop was Guam Regional

Medical City in Dededo, where the sole survivor of the incident was being treated. Although in a coma, he needed to see this man and reassess the situation.

When he emerged from the baggage bay and exited G.I.A., he was surprised to see a short line of yellow taxis waiting on the street. The taxis looked commercial. *Guam is a popular tourist destination for Americans,* he reminded himself, often surprised when traveling abroad. One of the cars moved into the lane and waved him over. The driver shifted into park mid-lane and jumped out to open the door for his passenger. Alex greeted the driver.

"Hospital, please." Alex said, handing the driver a printout of the written address.

He was puzzled when the cabbie responded with, "Yes, Sir, Mr. Joe, Sir."

Alex's brow furrowed in confusion, but then he thanked him. As the car sped away, he noticed the city looked deserted. Not abandoned but asleep, with all the restaurants and shops closed. The driver saw his observation and explained,

"Church day! Rest Day," he grinned. It was Sunday night.

After this, Alex noticed an obscene number of ornate little churches along the way. He saw a few people lazily wandering around a grassy area in the fading daylight, but otherwise, the city was quiet. The trip was quick and uneventful. Alex dozed for a few minutes, his head bobbing during the second half of the drive, but he sat up alert when he felt the car come to a sudden stop in front of GRMC. He was pleased to see an impressive, five-story hospital that looked to be newly built, no more than five years old.

"Thank you, Driver," he said, nodding and handing up his fare plus a twenty-dollar tip, which the driver took with hesitation.

Alex disembarked, realizing he should've checked into his room first, as he now had to carry his luggage through the hospital. Still, haste took precedence over appearances, especially since the man was in a coma. He could probably crawl into the bed and nap on top of the guy for all he would care. Alex didn't think that Tracy, which was the guy's name, would mind if he carried a few bags.

Entering the hospital, he looked for any staff on duty. Although luxurious, no one seemed to be attending the front desk. His mind rewound about 15 seconds to the staff smoking socially by the dumpster; he considered that one of those women might be the front desk clerk on break. Live tropical plants decorated the walls and countertops, and one stern-looking maintenance worker, watering them, looked up, offering no help. A flatscreen on the counter showed a news anchor interviewing a young man in a sports uniform, with statistics scrolling across the bottom of the screen. A loud waterfall splashed in the foyer, and Alex looked around again. The maintenance worker continued to scowl directly at him.

"Now, to you, Stephanie," the silver-haired gentleman on the screen said to the young, fresh-faced anchor. "Thank you, Jeff." she replied, looking pleasant but appropriately alarmed by the upcoming event. Taking another look around, Alex noticed that all the signs were in English. He spotted one that read, "Intensive Care Unit," and assumed that hall was as good as any. Crouching to retrieve his belongings, a feminine voice called out from the front doors. A woman of tiny stature, not exceeding four feet nine, with a very full figure, toddled past him and behind the counter, nearly out of sight. She smoothed her hair, tucking a few unruly strands back into a massive bun, and took up her post behind the counter, never breaking eye contact. She tucked a small cigarette purse under the counter into a drawer.

"Welcome to Guam Regional Medical City, Dededo, where we offer world-class medical care to the residents of Guam and the CNMI, Palau, the FSM, and the Marshall Islands, including all of Micronesia. Our Specialty Clinics include Cardiology, Oncology/Hematology, Hyperbaric Wound Care, Neurology, Orthopedics, Pulmonology, Infectious Disease Control, and other departments like Radiology, Patient Education, Physical Medicine & Rehabilitation, and Emergency." She took a long breath and added a disarming smile. "How may I help you?". He smirked in return, refreshed by her energy.

He'd found her performance entertaining and her strong command of the language reassuring. Furthermore, he felt that she would be more than adequate to guide him in the direction he needed.

"Yes. I hope you can. I'm looking for a patient named Tracy John from the United States. Can you tell me where I might find him? He was admitted yesterday after a terrible accident at sea and, sadly, is in deplorable condition," he elaborated with almost all of the information at his disposal.

"Tracy John? Can you tell me his date of birth, Sir?" she inquired as her very long fingernails made a pleasant clacking sound on the surface of a flatscreen monitor at the reception station.

"I can. Give me a moment," he responded walking away from his luggage and approaching the counter, briefcase in hand, thumbing his reports.

"No need, Sir. I have found him. He is in the Intensive Care Unit in bed 16," she said, pleasantly closing the program, her gaze lifting to him from beneath long, dark lashes. "That's a private room," she added, brightening his mood with another warm smile.

"Do you need to see my ID?" he offered, in no hurry to pick up his heavy bags and walk down a long corridor to stare at some vegetable at the behest of his employer.

"No, Sir. The hospital campus is open to the public, as we treat many outpatients and their families. However, you will be asked to show identification on the floor before gaining access to the patient's room. The hall you need is… right that way," she responded as she stepped out from behind the counter and pointed down the hall he initially intended to take. Nodding in appreciation, he now felt properly attended to.

After verifying his identity and intended business regarding the patient at the nurse's station, he was granted access to room 16. He was surprised to see an attendant dropping off dinner to an upright patient who appeared quite lively and spoke Tagalog to the nurse. Alex stepped back and double-checked the room number. Slightly puzzled, he entered.

"I'm Alexander Becker, Quality Control, Safety, and Environmental Manager of Dominion Petroleum Corporation, looking for Tracy John?" he began.

"I am him," he said in thickly accented English.

"I'm happy to see you looking so well." Alex held out a hand to shake with the tentative young man, approaching one of the chairs at the bedside. Tracy weakly returned the shake and nodded toward the chair, permitting him to sit.

"I am alive. No one else is," he responded. "So, I guess I am more than well."

"Yes. It was reported to corporate you were… incapacitated."

"I am not," he testified.

"Yes," Alex agreed apologetically, deliberately avoiding phrases that contained the word *sorry* because that could be misconstrued as an admission of guilt or negligence. "Can you tell me what your position was on the rig?" he queried, poised over a legal pad with a ballpoint pen in hand. Tracy looked over the bed rail at this man, conveying a severe lack of faith in his superior.

"Don't you know this? I was the lead geologist assigned to semi-submersible platform K. The reports I had studied indicated that this site was safe for drilling. The reports were wrong, the trench was not safe!" he illuminated, indignation rising in his voice. "I had recruited my little brother to come and work on that barge. He'd only joined me two weeks ago. I was so busy prepping for the first drill that I had only seen him once."

"My condolences for your loss, Mr. John. May I have the name of your brother and his position?" The air hung heavily between them. Alex waited, hoping his meeting wouldn't be fruitless; he didn't have any words that felt appropriate to say to this young man who'd fought so hard on behalf of Dominion. What it cost him was immeasurable. Alex felt the tug to be less formal and instead be present on behalf of mankind, not the firm; however, duty called, and he remained silent.

Tracy lifted the dome covering his entrée, and He shook his head when he saw the food choice.

"Kelaguen uhang," he said in frustration. When this didn't register with the businessman, Tracy explained, "This is a dish of shrimp and prawns."

"Not your favorite?" Alex guessed.

"I'm deathly allergic to shellfish. I'm the only survivor of the explosion, and the hospital staff nearly murdered me in my sickbed! What kind of hospital is this?" he asked, sitting up, grimacing, looking into the hall probingly.

"Explosion?" Alex asked with interest, then changed his tone. "Can I get you something else to eat? They have a cafeteria. What would you like?" he offered, as if a crusty, non-lethal, cafeteria dinner might cure all the man's ails.

The phone blared to life, shattering the silence. Realizing his IV cord tethered him too closely to his cot to answer, Tracy's hands clenched into fists, looking over his shoulder.

"Allow me." Alex offered, picking up the canary yellow receiver. "Hello. Room of Tracy John. May I help you?

"Kapatid? Buhay ka pa? Big brother, umiiyak si mom!" said a frantic girl on the other end of the line.

"Uh… It's for you," he said, covering the receiver. "What would you like for dinner? I'll go while you talk," he suggested.

"Adobo," answered Tracy dismissively. "Please, give me the phone," he said with a wave, dismissing the strange man and beginning a conversation with a welcome, familiar voice.

"Masama ang pakiramdam ko, Angel. Ang sakit ng ulo ko." Pulling the phone away from his ear, he said, "My brother's name was Jasir," and then resumed his conversation with his sister. Alex frowned upon hearing that, noticing that the young man was probably delivering the news of Jasir's death to a family member. He knew that Dominion did not have a complete list of the fatalities. Alex was surprised to learn during his phone call that Jasir was not on the list and that they were only updating the records monthly to the cloud. There might be as many as 200 bodies lost at sea that they had no record of. As he looked around the cafeteria, he also called the home office.

"I was told this guy was an American laborer," Alex argued with the woman in records. He's from Manila, but he has an American visa. "And he's a scientist, not a laborer."

"Everyone who works on the marine barge is listed as a laborer except the foremen. They are coded by pay grade. Everyone on the platform was on a pay scale 'G,' except for the foreman and service workers," she explained unapologetically. With no further information than before, he concluded his call and tried to order some adobe for Tracy. None could be found, so he settled for a turkey sandwich, a fruit bowl, and a strawberry frappe. *Who doesn't love strawberry?* He reasoned. He returned to the ICU with his spoils, hoping the snacks would lighten the mood. Tracy was off the phone and ready to talk. Alex noticed the man's swollen red eyes and the tissues on the bed. His gut twisted.

"There are things you need to know," Tracy said as he reached for the food.

"They didn't have any adobe," Alex explained with a slight frown as he handed Tracy the food. "And the kitchen was closed, but they did have some prepackaged stuff, and a barista was on duty. No shellfish!" He promised, hands raised, palm up as if in a stickup. Tracy shook his head in mild disgust at this man's lack of cultural awareness, having never heard of adobo, and stated the following.

"Get out your notepad." Tracy opened the dry sandwich wrapper and sipped noisily on the frappe. "On 'D' Day, the day of the explosion, I was on a dinghy half a mile from the drilling site, pulling some samples. For the last three months, the marine team has assembled the drill below with new machinery. Do you know anything about the Mariana Trench?" he asked. Alex opened his mouth to reply, but didn't have anything groundbreaking to reveal, so he chose not to speak. The scientist continued.

"This place has been less explored than the moon. It's an amazing mystery, geologically speaking and otherwise. It's like a scar in the

Earth's crust that's deeper than Mount Everest is tall. Since it's become a Marine National Monument, I don't see how you were able to get permission to drill for crude oil," he digressed in disgust. Alex held up a hand to interject.

"I do know that. See, not the whole trench is protected, and we agreed to finance some environmental research, which might have been why you were there," Alex supplied. Tracy cut him off.

"I was watching the team because when the drill started, the surface of the water began to vibrate. The supervisors were directly above topside, on a boat with monitors gauging the depth of the drills. Most everyone was out on the platform watching. This day was one we had all worked toward for the last eighteen months.

We had just completed the connection of the main umbilicus the week prior. You know every face on the rig when you work and live with the same 500 people for over a year. It should've taken about five hours to breach the crust, but after about a minute of boring, it happened. That was the moment of impact, of what, I don't know. I was knocked unconscious and nearly drowned. Luckily, I had a life jacket and was tethered to my boat.

When I awoke afloat near my vessel, I observed that the men in the boat were atop a giant geyser, parts of them and their boat were. Everyone on the barge was watching, yelling. A second boom sounded, creating a massive tidal wave. This caused the barge to tip and bob up and down on the water. I heard explosions from there, and watched in disbelief when it began to catch fire."

"Two blasts, fire on the platform,' Alex scrawled.

"I watched people jump to their deaths. I heard the screams of those burning and watched others dismembered airborne as explosions blew up one after another. I sat, horrified, knowing that they were all lost, including Jasir. I knew I was unlikely to be found. "Last night, someone spotted me floating several miles from the rig. A pilot of a—" he struggled for the word, "—jet, and brought me here. I've been thinking about what went wrong since." He swallowed, taking a sip from his drink before going on.

"I figured the drill must have punctured an undetected cavern, creating a vacuum, causing the geyser. I believe the blast generated a wave that ruptured the gas lines. Next, the compression tanks on the rig burst. When those ignited, it set off a chain reaction. Because of my position, I was blown clear of the field of destruction and floated away," he paused, wiping his eyes, his voice cracking. "I hesitated to take this job because I'm not a marine geologist, but the pay was good. I planned to marry my fiancé this fall, and the money would have gone a long way toward our honeymoon. My working theory is that this pocket was formed by magma at least three million years ago, which cooled too quickly, resulting in the formation of a cavity. Due to the intense pressure of the cavern, it was believed that retrieving it would require less energy, but the huge release of pressure wasn't accounted for. Our calculations were based on estimated factors.

That was all a working theory since no one had ever drilled for oil so deeply. There was no way to know exactly what would happen. He looked up at Alex and saw him checking his phone to make sure it was still recording.

"Invaluable information," Alex volunteered, holding up the phone.

"As I watched the geyser, I saw gelatinous forms emerging from below. They flowed with the water and then spread across the surface like plasma, shapeless. Initially, I thought they were the liquefied remains of jellyfish, but I saw membranes forming into groups. They had no distinct body parts but seemed to attract each other. Before the second blast, I observed several masses forming, unlike anything I've seen before; we might have transported a new species from the depths to the surface. I don't know how it could survive above if it's biologically adapted for life on the ocean floor, but interfering with nature can have unexpected outcomes. Maybe it's a top predator of amoebas and microorganisms in the trench depths. We should try to document their development—or their demise," he remarked, finishing the last pieces of ice from the plastic sphere containing the watery frappe.

"Well, that was a lot of information!" Alex exclaimed with raised eyebrows. "First and foremost, I am glad that you do appear, alive. Secondly, how much of this account would you feel was an indisputable fact? Would you say there were two separate blasts?" Alex pressed.

Tracy shrugged in disbelief. “You know, I’m exhausted. I don’t really want to talk anymore today,” he said, as he lay back in his bed. He raised his head when Nurse Jones entered the room.

“Sir, I’m so sorry, but our visiting hours are over now. You may come tomorrow.” The blond nurse instructed. She stood there stiffly, noting Alex’s lack of response.

“Of course!” he relented. "Thank you so much for all your help. I’ll be in touch. Here’s my card. Please contact me directly if you need anything or have any questions," he said to Tracy as he gathered his luggage, leaving one card by the phone. "And thank you for *your* help!” he said to the nurse. “He looks well,” he said to her over his shoulder as he exited the room. She stood blinking for a moment, then turned to tend to her patient.

Alex left the infirmary wondering about the implications of this and the unfortunate death toll. *How did they know that no one else was left alive?* he wondered. He needed to see for himself. While en route to his hotel, he uploaded the recording to the cloud, booked a chopper, and emailed Townsend an update. He set down his belongings, washed and shaved his face, ordered a sandwich from room service, and took a taxi to the helipad.

"Becker," he introduced himself to the pilot.

"Cairo," the dark-haired pilot responded. Alex took note of the man's youthful, gold-flecked eyes and wondered how old the kid was. "You need to fly over the Mariana Trench?" he asked. Alex buckled his seatbelt and put on his headset to communicate over the roar of the blades. The glossy craft had already begun its ascent. He fitted his headset over his ears, adjusted the mouthpiece, tapped it, and then explained what he was hoping to see in more detail.

"Yes, Sir," the pilot acknowledged in compliance. "I hope you're not looking for survivors. There's not much left out there." Alex nodded, verifying that he'd heard the man but indicated that he needed to decide that for himself. The aircraft sliced through the aerosphere cleanly with ease. "We'll be there in fifteen minutes," Cairo remarked, turning his head in Alex's direction for just a moment and then falling quiet as he meditatively maneuvered the craft. The copter rose and dipped with the grace and agility of a bird of prey, riding the zephyr like a gentle roller coaster.

As they left the coast, Alex saw unidentifiable debris floating. As they flew over the barge, he was shocked to see that it was bobbing, not lopsided, but entirely upside down. He had been told that under no circumstances could that occur. The force needed to flip a platform of that size did not exist in nature. He instructed the pilot to fly as low as possible and examined the charred remains of more than one individual or parts of several people. The cadavers were now very waterlogged, and he suddenly began rethinking shoveling down that meal he'd hastily eaten before he left. He was even more surprised to see the geyser that Tracy had described still flowing, but with less force.

It was now bubbling over the area, which must have been where they punctured the cavity. Cairo drove the scene in circles until they'd burned through their fuel. Alex gave a thumbs up, authorizing a return to shore. As they lifted, he noticed a sheen on the water's surface in an area. Not an oil slick, but something else

"Hey? What is that?" he asked the pilot, pointing.

"I don't know. Fish or something," he replied with zero interest, his goal remaining to return to shore before they ran out of gas. Alex assessed that it was vast as they gained more height, a big, shimmery sheet. It was impossible to determine its size. Maybe 100, maybe 1,000 feet wide. He got out his phone and began filming. Tightening his seatbelt, he leaned over the edge of the copter, recording and instructing, "Stay here a minute, nice and low." The pilot rolled his eyes, double-checking his gauges.

"Yeah, Joe," he obeyed. Alex could only tell where the thing was on the surface of the water. He could only see it when the sun reflected off of it because it was translucent. *Maybe it's a type of algae,* he thought, trying to grasp any familiar concept. Looking around, he considered ways to gather more information. The ocean suddenly dropped lower and lower beneath them as they rose, making anything in the water invisible even to his camera lens. This might be what the geologist saw, but it was massive. Alex noticed a pebble on the floorboard of the aircraft.

"Hey, drop as low as you can," he instructed.

"Just for a minute, man. We're out of time,"

the pilot informed him.

“Yeah. Fine.” He was already exhausted and eager for this workday to end. Cairo descended quickly; Alex was almost free-falling. The pilot chuckled at the foreigner's obvious discomfort.

“That's as low as I can go. It burns fuel to rise and fall,” Cairo explained, raising his palms up and down. Nodding, Alex turned back toward the water and hit record again. He dropped the rock, recording the descent as it hurtled down toward the center of the mass. As the rock drew near, the creature leaped up and grabbed the rock, devouring it. It reacted biologically, he observed, amazed. It took the form of a complex animal with jaws or limbs, then unassimilated just as quickly

CHAPTER TEN

Mermaids

HATTIE AND JUSTINE, two young school teachers, enjoyed a day out on Grandfather Lyon's sailboat, soaking up the last bit of summer on the Pacific Coast. Their kids, aged three, five, and six, ran the deck with the excitement of a summer's day on the gently rocking sea.

"Hadley, get back from that edge!" her mother called, looking over the top of her sunglasses from her sunny spot on the deck, her drink nearly spilling over the edge of her highball.

"Mama, the water is so shiny," Hadley observed. Little Gracie Lane toddled over with big brother Daxon hot on her heels, looking over the edge of the Napa Valley Wildflower, sticking fingers through the lifeline netting installed just for them.

"Stay back from the water, or you guys will have to play inside the cabin," Christine warned from her lounge chair, golden skin glistening with oil, careful not to ding her wet nail polish.

"Yes, Mama." Gracie nodded as the kids ran back to their game of catamaran. The two women relaxed, listening to the kids squeal with laughter from a distance as they gossiped about their awkward principal and her new suspected love interest.

"I could tell from the day we had that welcome meeting," Hattie explained, swishing around her drink. "I always sensed something funny going on between those two." Chris giggled, enraptured by the carefree leisure of her first summer vacation as a teacher while soaking up the sun, knowing this precious time was all theirs.

"Oooh! Look at this tan line!" Christine announced as she pulled her bathing suit strap off her tawny shoulder.

"Golden Goddess!" Hattie exclaimed seductively, fluttering her eyelashes dramatically and gulping down the contents of her glass. Giggling, she jumped up to pour another, still giggling at her own hilarity.

"What about me?" Christine crooned, standing up, gulping her last sip, and releasing her damp thighs from her sweaty, sun-blasted seat. As the ladies headed down the steps to get crushed ice and find another bottle, the water nearby glimmered inexplicably.

Dase laid out a small blanket for the girls near the stern of the boat. While lying on their sun-kissed bellies, the two girls nibbled on cheddar cheese cubes and a bunch of grapes. With their mouths full, the children casually discussed the sparkling water. Dason hopped up and ran off.

"The sparkling water is where mermaids come… come to sing songs to real men," Gracie speculated. "Yeah. But," she began again, having another thought, "—they're not scary!" she assured her rapt audience with a flourish of chubby fingers.

"Well, I think that the sparkle water…." Hadley supplied, squinting in deep thought.

"What water?" Dason asked, rejoining the conversation after coming back from peeing off the port side.

"That glitter water!" Grace pointed just off as he wiped his damp hands on his trunks before diving back into the snacks.

"Well, why is the water so twinkly?" Dason asked, stretching out his fingers and clenching his fists to show the sparkle—a tiny stream of grape juice running from the gap where he had a missing front tooth, the new one just starting to grow in his top gum.

"It's 'cause of the mer- mermaids. The fis- - " Hadley's words fell away as she peered at the iridescent sheet through caramel tresses blowing across her face in the breeze. While the children chattered, the gelatinous blob stretched out into an extensive sheet, thinning. They fell silent as they observed a seagull land directly onto the mat. It dipped but didn't tear as the bird settled onto it to preen. The hen lifted a wing and tucked her beak underneath, separating her feathers with the ridges in her beak, removing the tough sheaths from her newly molted feathers. She diligently pulled and spat out the debris a few times before tucking her head back under to fluff out her down. As the bird twisted her neck to clean up the feathers on her mantle, Hadley took a step closer to the aft, curiously noticing one area of the aqueous carpet creeping up in a silent wave. Eyes widening, she saw that the glimmering sheet had begun to take shape. Suddenly nervous and unable to speak, she reached out for Dason, keeping both eyes fixed on the creature. He was still sitting, asking his sister about her fish people. Stretching, Hadley found his forearm and, speechless, tugged.

Gracie and Dason both turned to look out at the water. The shimmering blanket suddenly became wildly predacious. The flat film took the form of a razor-toothed carnivore, voracious jaws, folding the bird in half in one bone-breaking crunch and pulling her under the sea before she could struggle or release any more than a gargled call of alarm. A single down feather was left floating in the air where she had been. The children peered, frozen, leaning over the railing while the cocoon, just under the water's surface, appeared to be masticating the still living fowl, blood spurts emanating from the broil. Baffled sounds of struggle, oxygen bubbles, and gore escaped the chrysalis, seeping into the ocean water. Meal devoured, the gelatinous creature resumed its unassuming, glassy, flat form, only detectable by the sheen cast on the water's surface.

"Mom! Mommy! Mama!" The children ran shrieking to their mothers, tumbling down the steps into the safety of the cabin, trying to relay the horrifying tale, killing the women's buzz in an instant. Dason's lime green sunglasses, which had fallen from his sweaty brow, dropped into the water. They floated slowly downward through a sun-dappled depth, surrounded by a milky cloud released by the blob. The glasses were quickly engulfed and fused with nearby life forms and minerals to form a significant mass that swiftly sank into the deep, dark depths.

CHAPTER ELEVEN

Hoofstock

IT WAS A BLAZING MORNING in Fairfield, North Dakota. John watched the sun creep over the horizon from his vantage point on the front deck, illuminating the landscape. He sipped his steaming cup of black coffee, his lips pursing slightly after each bitter sip as was his Saturday ritual. Mug emptied, he walked out to the feed barn to tend to the livestock. Hearing grasshoppers colliding with his denim overalls, he rustled through the wild wheatgrass and clover. The tall man with a strong build watched as the flying insects began to come alive, moving over the flowers and native grasses, crawling and buzzing around. He thought about what the neighbor said regarding all the lakes being higher than they'd ever been in recorded history, and thought deeply on the subject.

He was a rugged man. His slightly shaggy hair fell over his hazel eyes as he leaned down into the feed bags. He scooped out a swine pellet and pulled off six flakes of alfalfa and half a Folgers tin of sweet feed. His broad back worked as he stood with nearly half a bale of hay on his shoulder and the few canisters of meal hanging in beat-up buckets from calloused hands. He squinted as dust and debris from the hay wafted around him, his mind still elsewhere.

Noisy oinks and slurps roused him back to his chores. He beamed at the fat, spotted sow and ravenous piglets, eleven in this litter. He thought back to when Mother Pig was a greedy little piglet herself. She had come to them as an orphan. Josie and Nicolas had bottle-fed her day and night. That piglet screamed her head off when ready for her bottle. Chuckling at that memory, he tossed the swine fodder into the stall.

Sarah, the robust dappled sow, and her piglets rooted and snorted in delight at the delivery. He leaned over the splintered goat pen to drop in the hay and a pinch of grain. Next, he entered the horse barn where Hondo, the Mustang, Buttermilk, the creamy Welsh Pony, and Beau, the old bay thoroughbred, stood quietly waiting for their breakfasts. Hondo approached the feeder, swatting at the mosquitoes with his tail. Buttermilk whinnied excitedly, and Beau snickered quietly. The man placed his large, warm hands on the face of the bay, his old friend. He looked deeply into the large, round eyes of this animal, and they looked back into his, almond irises reading into the depths of the farmer's sepia gaze.

"I know," John said aloud, firmly patting the horse's muscular neck. "Nic will be back soon, and then he'll be feeding you again. And you want food, don't you?" the man acknowledged, chuckling, realizing that, really, he was talking to himself. The giant horse nickered again, seeming to understand. He picked up three flakes of hay and dumped the sweet-smelling grain into the big horse's trough. He gave the mustang two flakes, and the pony got one. They each got to work quickly. He reached for the pony's neck. Little Buttermilk had been his son's barrel horse when he was a kid, although he'd outgrown him since. Besides, the boy didn't have much time for riding or spending time with the livestock these days. Like all the teens in the area, he planned his thrilling escape from Bumfuck, Nowhere. His dad understood. He knew his son wanted to see the world. And so, with his winter bonus, he bought two tickets for a Caribbean cruise for his wife and son at his wife's insistence.

"He's seventeen now," she argued. "We don't have much time left with him before he leaves, and if we end on a low note, he might not come back here to visit his folks once he's gone," Josie said. The couple were honest and hardworking people who loved their son. This seemed like a sad truth. That Christmas, the family gift was for mother and son to go on a cruise the following summer. That was a gift Nic was excited about. He couldn't believe that his best friend couldn't go, but his dad told him he could make new friends on the ship. It would be for seven days. Maybe he'd even meet a girl, he suggested.

After swimming through the sea of crickets heading back to the house, John sat at his computer to check his email. He received a notification that his cloud storage was full. He wondered how that could be, since he'd just upgraded his package. *Did someone dump their entire device?* He bristled. That'd happened the last time Nic switched cell phones. John opened the files and, surprised, started looking through the photos and videos from the cruise—pictures of Nickie and Josie at the restaurant eating exotic seafood. Nicolas is climbing a rock wall. A short video of him swimming and Josie lying in a lounge chair in her bathing suit with her hair in curlers. She said she planned to see a magic show that first night, but the kid didn't want to go. He'd rather stay by the pool. After that, he smiled at the various selfies they each took. A photo of Josie alone in a casino, Nic eating hot wings with a group of boys around his age. Nic and a girl on the upper deck watching the sunset, his arm comfortably slung over her shoulder. The ocean seemed to stretch on forever. Then there was another video. Nicolas was on the ship's prow with another girl, pointing out the huge wake the boat left behind. Some little kids were horsing around nearby. The girl left his side to join her family.

"Hey, but what's your name? I'm Nic!" he called after her. His dad chuckled at his son's persistence. The camera panned out to the water, where the wildlife was putting on a show. He heard some passengers talking about dolphins, but as Nic's camera zoomed in, John saw that those were blue whales leaping frantically. With the phone's zoom focusing better than the human eye, the camera lens could see a massive creature chasing them. The giant broke the water's surface; jaws open wide with razor-sharp teeth. In a breathtaking spiral, following the whale's arc, jaws still open, she clamped down on the back two-thirds of a whale with incredible force, like a bear trap, and landed gracefully back in the ocean with almost no splash. John rubbed his eyes and refocused on the footage. An eerie silence fell as the ship's passengers leaned over the railing, frozen.

The water around the area was quickly ensanguined as the sapphire water turned purple with lifeblood—so much blood. The scene had unfolded a few hundred feet from the ship as people began to look at each other, befuddled. A colossal fin broke the water, approaching the bow, and then resubmerged. The center of the ship made a loud cracking sound. The impact of the blow knocked passengers off their feet. Screaming and cries erupted as vacationers ran, seeking the safety of their loved ones. Others fell to their feet, clinging to the railing—a few dove for shelter.

The ship split down the center, with the fault line crawling up the vessel's keel. The weight shifted, knocking people further off balance. The pound of gushing water instantaneously filled their ears as they took on water. Frantic shrieking escalated as the spray rocketed up toward them. The crack in the hull snapped and echoed loudly. The ship broke in two, attached loosely by a thin band of metal; the two ends quickly became waterlogged in the center, causing the ship's ends to slowly stand upright. People clung to life, murmuring prayers and pleas for help.

John watched the scene unfold in disbelief, knowing he would never see his wife and child again. His fists clenched and unclenched as he considered that he had sent his family off to suffer this death sentence by buying those tickets against his better judgment, but they'd desperately wanted to go.

As he waited for them to sink slowly into the waters, the death machine lurking, a colossal shadow loomed in the depths. Suddenly, it burst from the ocean like a torpedo. Spinning up and over the ship, tail oscillating as if she were swimming through the air. She landed aboard with the force of an earthquake, rupturing water lines and creating a geyser that erupted from the terrace. Onlookers watched the scene unfold in astonishment. She snapped the observation deck, thrashing, obliterating wood, metal, and flesh in her path. With one flip of her tail, she smashed the visitor's information center, sending mangled passengers sprawling into the sea. She writhed, looking at the ship's bow with one enormous, acrimonious eye.

Her thick cartilaginous sclera intelligently darted the rods and cones: seeking. With one powerful wave of her body, she collapsed the top deck, crushing those praying for refuge below. Screams erupted, and fires ignited in the engine room; the craft quickly took on water. Those still watching were perplexed by the fact that this shark no longer appeared the slate gray that she first appeared to be, but more of the teak color of the deck, and on this 1200-foot ship, she seemed to take up over half the vessel. This wasn't possible, of course, but there she was. She began to convulse wildly, collapsing levels upon levels of the ship as she sank, finally shattering the craft into countless pieces and plummeting violently back into the swell, the death toll rising with each whip of her tail.

Nic and his camera went over the railing. In the last seconds of the footage, his father could hear him wailing. The camera plummeted downward, submerged, and bubbles trailed skyward before the footage went black. This was the end.

John sat on his gingham couch motionless, unable to speak, think, or process anything he'd just seen. Outside, the world kept turning. The birdsong continued. The breeze tugged at the wildflowers. A large, sapphire-eyed dragonfly with ruby wings settled on the screen door, resting up for its afternoon mosquito hunt, curiously peering into the house and watching the man as he wept.

CHAPTER TWELVE

No Touchy

~ Two Weeks Later ~

UNBELIEVABLY, ANTON was chiding himself for his ultimate lack of resolve in offering Rukia snacks. Smiling proudly at his strange little dog perched happily on the office chair next to him, he decided he'd made the right choice in accepting this job. He was hired as the Chief Cyber Data Analyst for the Department of

Defense, not the Pentagon. Well, really, it was this or incarceration, but this was working out just fine. Especially when Rukia looked at him with those runny little eyes, she had her pup tent on the cushy chair to his left so he could pet her and offer treats while still keeping one hand flying across the keyboard.

He now had a large corner office next to the boundless processors he'd ordered. Mysteriously, this half-million dollars' worth of equipment was billed to the jerk who had made him eat pavement when he was taken into custody. Anton now had an enormous glass desk with a dozen monitors and split screens to view several feeds at once. It was ten in the morning, he noted. With a click of one button, all screens merged into one. Time to watch Netflix and have lunch. True, he took an early lunch, but he worked best in spurts. He took a second lunch at 1:00, then took Rukia for a walk at 2:30, and often didn't return to the office until the next day. That was until he got into a flow; then, sometimes, he would work for 36 hours straight without coming up for air. Given the freedom to work however he pleased, he actually liked this job. And the salary! Wow! There were a lot of zeros in that paycheck! The best perk, besides being allowed a canine companion, was immunity from any law he may have broken in the past, present, or future, thanks to the fine print in the hacked version of his contract. He could work remotely if he wanted, but at this point, why would he? His subsequent demand was to be isolated from all colleagues except for one. No one else was allowed to interact with him. He had no dress code and no obligation to socialize. Furthermore, he could set his own hours. He had a fridge in his office, his own water cooler, and all the processing power a guy could dream of.

He was assigned a personal assistant, a 20-something MIT grad. He liked her. Her name was short and no-nonsense: Dru. She was very pretty, with large doll-like eyes, about 5′6", curly hair, and impeccably dressed, but Anton was oblivious to all of that. Her assistant was an AI named FROLO. She had told him what the acronym stood for, but he dismissed that information immediately, not caring. Anton liked FROLO because he didn't talk or have eyes that you had to stare at like people wanted you to. He was essentially a skeletal frame with various tools at his disposal. The robot reminded Anton of a Swiss Army knife that could do math and deliver snacks. FROLO was reliable, and Dru wasn't bad either. She could read a room and, for the most part, Anton didn't notice whether she was there or not. When he needed something, she brought it. Basically, she understood him well enough not to interrupt his process. Little did he realize that she kept regular office hours and mostly worked alongside him, running algorithms from a small desk on the other side of the room. She even had her own formula to predict when he might need a break or a snack. Her predictions were about ninety-five percent accurate after day five. She created a digital choice board to suggest breaks and snacks, warding off decision fatigue. Her system was working perfectly.

After he came in six days in a row, wearing the same stretched-out clothes, she ordered him replicas of the T-shirt and sweatpants. She had them laundered and prepared for him to change into when he arrived, but he touched them once and said those new clothes made his "hair tickle." That concept she didn't follow, but she respected it nonetheless. She nearly giggled aloud when he finally tried them. He dropped his drawers right in front of her, bum exposed, no underwear. Tittering, she turned away and went back into her corner office to give him some privacy. She sent FROLO to retrieve the dirty ones so they could be washed and returned. Her feelings of delighted victory soon changed when she saw that his productivity had decreased by 80 percent. The next two days were marked by excessive coughing and throat clearing throughout the day, which she documented as some of the tics indicating elevated stress levels.

It's no wonder he looks the way he does, she lamented, feeling a bit guilty for judging him.

This kid was a savant whose abilities exceeded his superior's understanding. Though he was odd, he wasn't unhinged. Carefully raised by loving parents who sheltered and nurtured him with kindness, he remained surprisingly humble. He never let power go to his head and followed a strict moral code. He occasionally used that energy for his own purposes, but it was all harmless.

Besides being slightly dog-obsessed and socially awkward, he was pretty balanced. More importantly, he could decipher codes at a glance with the aid of his eidetic memory, but he still possessed a rational understanding, unlike most people who were either cursed or blessed with his gifts. He was an astounding statistician and had an uncanny ability to connect unrelated facts and puzzle pieces to gain insight. With unlimited resources, it did not take him long to piece together the big picture of what was occurring on a global scale. With access to all information from the internet, radio, phones, CCTV, security footage, drones, and satellite, he worked on something vital. Something that may be causing the end of everything as humans know it.

He'd been hired to solve a problem. He was told about a potential pandemic, a failed accident on the government's part; this virus was only supposed to escape a small area in 2020. It was meant to remain contained, revealing only small pockets of the population to scare the public into action. Well, that didn't go as planned. So, Plan B was to blame the Chinese wet food market. *Blaming the Chinese? How cliché,* he thought, being half-Chinese himself. Now, his job was to find a scientist who could develop a cure or at least a vaccine and to steer the media after the election.

Once he had the actual data about the crisis, he remained unfazed, knowing this rogue virus was less deadly than Influenza B or H1N1, which the human race had survived with little suffering. He waited a reasonable amount of time before suggesting a few vaccine recipes. He had hacked a voicemail from the scientist who secretly took credit for accidentally releasing the virus after drinking a whole 18-pack of beer while working late on Christmas Eve in Seattle. He planned to push for them to name it something personal, referencing that incident.

Suffering had followed, but too many people were on this crazy rock anyway. *I mean, that's nature's way. People were science's bitch. There was no way around it,* he thought.

However, since being given metaphorical keys to the castle, he followed a lead he'd been working on. A few things he'd seen had raised Rukia's hackles when he told her what he suspected. Of course, Rukia's hackles only rose because she was stretching, but this is how Anton worked through larger-than-life problems. His first task was to gather data, categorize it, and create a rating system for potential danger. The risk categories ranged from one to ten, with ten being the most severe, or world-ending. World governments spy through all tech. There was no 6-9 in Anton's system because there was no need, and he was not someone who wasted time, at least not in his mind. He had seen some things from a pinpoint perspective. But with his new level of omniscience, he had assembled a reel of footage: satellite images of a Philippine whaler's ship being decimated, a funny Snapchat posted by a college student, the private diary of a PR firm manager for an oil tycoon, a crazy epileptic priest, a raving native on a street corner talking about the ocean coming to get us or something, and then the disappearance of an entire cruise ship, all seemingly connected. He sensed a pattern, a chain of cause and effect, even if he hadn't figured out exactly how, but he believed it was escalating into something unprecedented—and not in a good way. *What should he do?* he wondered silently. He tilted his head and blinked, signaling his earpiece to dial phone extension #139.

"Michaels, I'm going to need a team."

CHAPTER THIRTEEN

Holy Trin

FATHER CHRISTOPHER JOHNSON ended his call with the Holy Trinity Roman Catholic Church Monsignor on 42nd Street in New York City. They'd discussed the Celebration of the Ascension of the Lord and the issue of the dwindling congregation. The clergy were under pressure from the archdiocese to grow the congregation, but despite attempts, people weren't coming. As the assistant priest, he was tasked with the dreadful job of recruiting new members. Additionally, he acted as the Executive Administrator for Academic Affairs at New York Theological Seminary, which kept him busy. Despite his focused apostolic pursuits, he'd felt spiritually isolated.

Vicars were assigned different jobs, and duties had been piling up as the number of priests dwindled. Father Dudley died unexpectedly from premature heart failure at age 37. Father Thomas chose to leave the Catholic Church and become a pastor so he could marry. Father Roman, who was 96, passed away peacefully in his sleep, although he'd not been active in service over the last several years.

For the past few years, Christopher had been going through a crisis of faith, a troubling separation from God. Throughout his life, he'd spent time worldwide bringing people hope through their walk with God. Seeing the miracle of salvation amid squalor renewed his faith in his youth. He thought it was time to travel abroad again, but he decided against it. Already in his late fifties, he was overweight and less energetic than he had been. The memory of trudging through the swamps in Haiti made him break out into a sweat.

He'd been lacking the divine inspiration he felt in his youth. As a result, he began to question his purpose in the church. For the past month, he'd been plagued by blinding migraines that left him debilitated; they started with tingling numbness in his right hand and an acrid taste on his tongue. These were signs of the pain to come. Grimacing at the taste and nervously flexing his hands open and closed, he grabbed his satchel, turned off the light switch with a thud, and decided to retire early for the day. It was already after four, and he knew he wouldn't be able to function for much longer. Reluctantly, he decided he'd better start walking. Taking deep breaths, he tried his best to stay calm. His goal was to reach his apartment in the clergy house without showing any signs of distress.

Heading down the path and shortcutting through the grass, he fumbled in his pockets for the old brass key. As he neared the rectory door, he saw stars as the blinding pain intensified. Usually, he relished this walk as he traversed the parish campus, enjoying the historic architecture of the ancient buildings, which contrasted with the bustling, sharp lines and modern feel of downtown. He appreciated the beauty of the climbing vines and the chirping sparrows making sport in the birdbaths. He admired the carefully sculpted gardens, but not today. Huffing, he closed the door. Hastily, he dropped his bag on the floor, kicked off his shoes, and fumbled toward his cot just as an ice pick hammered into his crown, knees buckling, and the contents of his stomach roiling. He grappled for the metal frame of his bed and heaved himself up, finding a brief moment of strength, knowing he could be incapacitated for hours. He closed his eyes, focused on his breathing, and, a moment later, began to convulse.

Sometime later, he was slowly awakened by the quiet chatter of two concerned voices. Turning over, he felt a damp towel slip from his face, causing the bright light of the harsh overhead to momentarily blind him. Detecting a faint taste of stomach acid in the back of his throat and the crust of vomit on his neck, he smacked his lips: sour. Reaching for the towel, he wiped his face and neck, carefully pushing himself up to sit. Blinking, the two men grew silent, watching Christopher rise. Quietly, they stood together, approaching him with caution.

“Christopher?” the Monsignor began. "Are you well?” he asked slowly. Dazed and weakened but no longer under duress, he was confused as to why an audience was in his apartment supervising him. Wiping his eyes, he noticed the sun coming in from the west window. The Monsignor continued, “Father Belli overheard you... He thought you were being attacked when you yelled. He used the master keys to enter and was surprised to find you catatonic, alone. He called me. We tried to wake you, and when we did, you sat up and started babbling. God's truth, Christopher, initially, we feared possession. After your fit, we agree it seemed more like a hallucinogenic delirium caused by fever."

"Fever?" Christopher questioned in complete confusion.

"Well, there was no fever, per se, but a sickness. We video-recorded the episode. Father Belli said that he had suspected something was amiss for a little while. He came to me two weeks ago, and I asked him to keep an eye on you. He already had permission to enter your suite when you didn't answer him at the door."

The ailing man's gaze traveled from one trusted friend to the other.

"Thank you, but I… I think I just need rest." He waved his hand, flicking fingers up in a gentle conveyance to excuse his guests for the evening.

"No," the Monsignor insisted. "Christopher, take a look."

The priest staggered to the empty seat in his tiny kitchenette, where a hot cup of tea sat on the sparse table. The phone, resting on a canister of sugar, began to play a two-minute video of him sitting motionless with his eyes wide open, uttering frantic words that were hard to understand. He seemed to be expressing the perspective of some intelligent creature in the sea. Based on what could be interpreted, he appeared to see through the eyes of a marine animal.

He rambled about how she, the immortal, is empathetic and seeks life forms. At first, she was just a baby, reborn from the explosion that had released her from her tomb. She emerged from the nest and instinctively began establishing her territory, floating, feeding, and swimming, growing, feeding, and devouring, her form evolving as she developed. Mother Earth was calling to her. No, to them, a whole fleet of them. Calling them to work. As they nursed and matured, they altered the sea through their life cycle.

Christopher apparently observed all this from the consciousness of a massive shark-like endoskeleton. A form unlike any modern shark.

It was so durable that it protected the animals from being crushed in the depths like a submarine, giving them a vast range. *What will happen to the land when most of the fish are gone?* He felt her wonder as she traveled, insatiable and driven. While in his fugue, he felt primal, ancient, only guided by instinct; his only clear conscious understanding was that *Mother was hurting*. Chris squinted, studying the footage as the fit seemed to ease.

"Mother is hurting. Mother is hurting. Mother… Yes. Mother…" speechless, he watched himself, babbling until his tensed body became lax, and he fell into a resting, dreamlike state.

"Christopher, you slept for many hours, unresponsive until you rolled over and regurgitated." His superior informed him, concerned.

"What is this all about?" Father Belli asked. "Have you been watching those science theory shows again? We called the rectory physician, and he explained this was likely a seizure, but agreed it was unusual. He mentioned you might have developed epilepsy. Stress can trigger uncontrolled electrical bursts in the brain's nerve cells, which can affect awareness. These can cause convulsions or impact our senses and emotions. He said this appeared to be a tonic-clonic seizure."

While listening to this apparent warning, Chris wiped his streaming eyes in embarrassment. The Monsignor gently laid a damp, cool towel on his forehead, unease flickering in his eyes. "Since you came in early and lay down, the doctor said this was probably not your first, and you're already familiar with the aura that precedes a seizure. Most unusual was that most people confuse their own experiences, not something that manifests outwardly." He kept talking. Chris was no longer paying attention. The Monsignor moved closer to the man, who was like a son, placing a clammy hand on his protégé's shoulder.

"Christopher, why hadn't you come to me if you were sick?" The priest asked quietly, looking grave. Before this, Chris had no memory of what happened afterward, only the dull glow of an ominous feeling. Now, after hearing his own ramblings, he remembered some of the visions firsthand. He knew one thing they hadn't realized yet—this world might be nearing its end. He wondered if the end of days he feared was real, not just a glitch caused by his epileptic brain. Why he felt this way, he couldn't say. Speechless, he said nothing. Seeing he needed rest, the Monsignor offered him comfort.

"Well, Son, you seem to be doing okay for now. I'm placing you on a three-day sabbatical. You have an appointment for testing at the hospital on Wednesday. We'll meet again after we get your results. Don't worry about anything right now—relax. Call Father Belli if you need anything. We'll handle your duties for now." He patted the man's chest, looking him in the eye, but Chris stayed despondent.

He managed a weak smile that encouraged the two men to trust it was safe to leave. He nodded acknowledgment and mumbled thanks as they departed, locking the front door behind them.

Momentarily, Chris stood, stripped out of his uniform, and went to take a shower. When the water turned warm, he stepped under the stream. As the water pelted him, he had sudden hair-raising flashbacks of his vision. He was... She: ravenous, powerful, searching, destroying our world one menacing mouthful at a time. He could feel her gaining strength, perilously aware of the plan, cognizant that this was not her first existence and would not be her last. His head sagged as the searing water fell upon him, exhausted but rationalizing that this vision must not have been accurate. He was sick, and the doctors would figure it out soon enough.

Holding onto that thought, he allowed the tension in his muscles to ebb. He bathed until the water turned arctic and then made himself a meager meal of Apple Cinnamon Instant Quaker Oats before turning out the light and sleeping like the dead.

CHAPTER FOURTEEN

Unexpected Company

"HURRY UP, YOU!" Evelyn said, rapping a friendly reminder on the bathroom door after noticing the pinging of the shower water still running.

"I have an eight o'clock class on Tuesdays," she smiled, reminding him, the intoxication from their reunion still absurdly fresh. She buttoned her blouse below her collarbone over a pale pink lace chemise, plucking modest diamond studs from her jewelry box. Fitting them into her ears instinctively, she gazed out the panoramic windows from their bedroom loft, admiring the wash of color as the sun peeked through the trees. Moving over to the armoire, she chose a vibrant scarlet blazer, pulling it over her stoic, white blouse, which was tailored to fit her petite yet curvy frame. She slipped her slender feet into a pair of dainty kitten heels, feminine but still practical for navigating the busy campus, nodding in satisfaction when she heard the telltale squeak of the shower knobs turning off.

She chuckled, hearing the damp towel snap in protest, and yanked it from the wall rack. She had to cover her mouth to keep from laughing out loud, listening to Adem groan loudly as he always did during his I-hate-mornings ritual. She glanced in the vanity mirror, artfully sweeping her hair into a large French twist-bun at her crown and securing it with two brass French pins, tugging loose the few tendrils that weren't entirely caught in the twist, allowing them to frame her face. She smiled softly, noticing how this classic style accentuated her distinctive mixed features, which she knew he especially appreciated. She checked her watch, ready to knock again to offer the current time along with her prediction for the traffic report. She paused, listening when she heard Kanik barking.

Stranger here, he was saying. She marched toward the sliding glass doors on the balcony, taking in the overhead view of three black SUVs out front with two suited men exiting from the first vehicle. She watched curiously, her brow furrowing with mild alarm. She called for Adem when she saw an armed man and woman with earpieces get out of the second vehicle, eying Kanik, taking stock of the perimeter. The first two mounted the stairs and began to approach the front door. The third pair looked as if they were going around back. As the wolf-dog heightened the alarm, the second car's driver made a hand signal to the passenger of the third vehicle. They were signaling to assist the second car, which approached from the high ground nearest the garage. Distracted by the gunmen, she was startled when warm water droplets dripped down her temple as a naked Adem towered over her, dampening the back of her jacket, peering over her shoulder.

"They look like government goons," he noted, fastening his well-fitted trousers. He shook out his curly hair, perturbed by their intrusion, he stretched his undershirt across his chest and over his head. Grabbing his tailored button-up, he swirled it behind him like a cape, pulling his arms in—left then right—as he descended the stairs barefoot to answer the knock at the kitchen door, the shirt unbuttoned. Staying just on his heels, Evie followed, increasingly intrigued by what they could want.

As he pulled open the door, the apparent leader removed his sunglasses, revealing a federal badge. "Doctor Adem James Humboldt and Doctor Evelyn Marie Humboldt?" he inquired, blazing blue eyes without any humor.

"Yes?" they replied in unison. He went on.

"I am Special Agent Clark with the U.S. Department of the Interior, Bureau of Safety and Environmental Special Circumstances. Special Agent Wager here is an Intelligence Analyst with the Federal Bureau of Investigation." The slender agent with a gun on her hip nodded in agreement. Her brown eyes narrowed as she took stock of the couple, jaw jutting with intensity.

"We have assembled a team," she said, "and you both need to come with us. This is an urgent matter of national security, which is all we can disclose at this time. You'll be more thoroughly debriefed when we reach our rendezvous."

"There is a chopper waiting at the top of the hill." Agent Clark conveyed.

"We've already informed the University of

Berkeley of your impending absence," Agent Wager added, Agent Clark nodding matter-of-factly, first to Adem and then to Evelyn. Agent Wager took a few steps back, putting her sunglasses back on, and concluding this declaration.

When the two remained unmoving, Agent Clark said, "We'll wait." He nodded respectfully, giving the doctors a moment to digest this information. Agent Wager conversed quietly with her double, allowing a few feet of privacy. He nodded and signaled something to the agents who waited below. The scientists stared at each other.

"Wait for what?" she leaned out, asking incredulously.

"Ma'am. You can't bring your dog, and you

might want to pack a bag." Agent Wager instructed the bewildered pair on what must be done next.

"I'll call Doc Smith to see if he has room in the clinic for a border. Pup needs his medicine," Adem said to his wife. Warmly, she put a hand on his shoulder in gratitude.

"I'll pack our bags," she stated in reciprocity, her body turning obediently, as her mind raced. Fifteen minutes later, they were given earmuffs and boarded an aircraft already primed for takeoff. One very concerned dog clearly objected to this avian swallowing his parents and flying them into the sky.

They started to rise from the Earth before their restraints were secured. In an instant, Evelyn saw an aerial view of their house, neighborhood, city, county, and then... clouds. They made the five-hour flight in two hours and forty-five minutes, a loud, chaotic ride. Their legs were numb when they landed, disembarking, ears ringing. Endorphins traveled through their veins, quickly making things feel more serious. They approached the Pentagon and were swiftly led into the National Military Command Center, a room not accessible to the public. The weight of what must be happening began to sink in.

CHAPTER FIFTEEN

Cadre

"DOCTORS, MEET THE TEAM," their crisply dressed escort announced as the couple was led to a table with other bewildered-looking men, women, and one kid.

I'm Michaels, the Pentagon's Director of International Crisis Resolution. "Everyone, these are Doctor and Doctor. Humboldt, the lead scientific investigators," he told the group.

Pointing to a strikingly handsome Filipino in his late 20s, he said, "This is Tracy John, the geologist present at what we now believe to be Exposure One."

Turning his gaze to a delicate-boned young woman dressed in a smart suit, he continued, "This is Emmie Longoria. She's a doctoral student in informational sciences with an existing Ph.D. in Media Research and Journalism. She has experience in data collection for investigations of this nature.

Alexander Becker, CEO of Quality Control, Safety, and Environmental Manager at Dominion Petroleum Corporation, appears to be responsible for initiating the release of the creatures. U

Upfront is Anton Isaac. He's our Cyber Data Analyst and Statistician. Though he is the youngest team member, he is also the coordinator and leader." Someone who could pass for a 15-year-old broke his gaze from some trance when he appeared to change a setting on his glasses. He stifled a snicker, indicating he was engaged in something humorous. He disengaged mentally, then wiped his nose, sniffing.

"Sorry. Replay of," he chortled. "Never mind! I'm here," he said, standing and waving one hand in a mock salute. "So, the researchers have arrived." He announced in a neutral tone to no one in particular. "Finally!" he muttered to himself. "I do believe that's everyone!" He proclaimed officially. "Alright!" he said, clapping. "Let's get started." He directed, taking his feet off the glass table, standing up. His demeanor shifted slightly to adopt a mild, authoritative stance.

"Long story short, our nation's public surveillance system includes an informational warning system. The scale is rated as follows: 1 – 5 for normal chatter. 1. How was your day 2. Discussions related to conflicts 3. Random talks about explosions, bombings, murders 4. Organized plans for violence with no capacity 5. Organized intent for school shootings, urban bombings, Unabomber, 9-11, and then there's 10, which is reserved for World War 4, nuclear war, or other global-ending events," he explained casually. "Yes," he confirmed, meeting the bewildered gaze of his audience.

Our government spies on all of us through any and all technology. Good people, right now, we are at a Ten." He paused, preparing to untangle the cyber web of a lifetime. Taking a deep breath, he looked at each member of this hand-picked group of intellects. "To bring you up to speed—" he interrupted himself. His mood visibly lightened. "Actually, let's start with lunch!" he decided, shifting tactics. "It's going to be a long day!"

After placing a group order at his favorite new hole-in-the-wall in DC, El Rinconcito Café, the questions started coming from various group members. Anton refused to entertain their inquiries and insisted they hold their questions until after his presentation. Only after lunch had been ordered did he show a horrifying video montage that summarized everything he believed was related to the current crisis, which he referred to as the Cataclysmic Megalodon Calamity, or the CMC.

While the smartly dressed, caramel-skinned assistant, Dru, unpacked their lunches, Anton began to unravel what he now knew from the bits of information his algorithm brought to his attention. He explained that the whole sequence started with the explosion on the rig. He pulled up sat footage and encrypted footage that belonged to Dominion Petroleum. He narrated what was unfolding as he displayed the images on several monitors to establish a comprehensive overview.

When the riggers breached that cavern, it punctured a hole in a pressurized cabin, causing a release with such force that it led to an explosion. Theoretically, this pocket was formed by the molten igneous rock that cooled too quickly, trapping oil and gas inside. Due to the high pressure of the vacuum, it was believed that retrieving it would require less energy. That was, in theory, since no one had previously extracted oil from such depths beneath the sea. When the drillers punctured the cabin, a geyser of water erupted with such force that it triggered an underwater explosion. TJ was blown clear of the main destruction zone in his boat, which floated adrift.

Turning and making eye contact with the geologist, he asked, "Is it okay if I call you TJ?" Without waiting for an answer, he continued. "I just like TJ. So, luckily, TJ, was fitted with a beacon device, which is how you were found drifting." He broke eye contact with the geologist and then addressed everyone. "He was the sole survivor from the crew on that rig. As the geyser finally lost force, a gooey substance was observed on the water's surface.

He next retrieved and projected the cell phone footage filmed by Becker, demonstrating that the masses had emerged from the cavern, grown, and expanded. They had assumed some form and were in three distinct clusters floating on the water's surface that, from a close-up angle, appeared to be aggressively absorbing phytoplankton. This, he surmised, was the embryonic form of the creature. He then pulled up the comical Snapchat footage of Hank and the good doctor. As soon as it was pulled up, Evelyn had her head in her hands and mumbled something. Adem gave her a supportive squeeze on her wrist.

"I knew it." She whispered to Adem, thinking about the talking she would give sweet Hank if she was ever permitted to return to regular life, which she was beginning to question. His theory was that the jellyfish-type animal was the fetal form of the same creature. Emmie covered her mouth in disbelief and amusement at the doctor seeing this clip.

Next, he pulled up some video recordings of a priest having a fit, during which he was croaking unintelligibly. He was foaming at the mouth and convulsing when, suddenly, he sat up wide-eyed and began reciting some deep-sea experience from a first-hand perspective of a monster. The most exciting part of this account was his clear explanation of the innate understanding he had of the animal, which seemed aware of her surroundings and even possessed a subconscious knowledge of what might come. From what they could interpret, he had omniscience about the beast. She was released from the cavern by Dominion. Man released the beasts, but nature stimulated their metamorphosis, birthing them again, as they did many eons ago.

Anton pulled up the following clip without any transition, a YouTube video posted by Donut Diggler Kid entitled 'crasey indiun n my street.' The shaky footage portrayed a young, dark-haired man sitting on a street corner as passersby left small bills, change, and various items at his feet. Initially, he appeared to begin meditatively chanting. This devolved into him pleading with the people of his city about a crisis that no one understood. Compassion for a man who seemed down on his luck compelled a few of them to offer their own alms to this spiritual envoy.

"In the past, my elders have foretold crises such as Smallpox, the Long Walk, and now a new virus. We must renounce our greed and perform the Ghost Dance once again. We must call on the favor of our spirit guides and grieve now for the Pretty Princess. She and her people have been lost and can never be recovered. She will not fall alone, my brothers and sisters. We shall all turn to ash together.

His mention of The Pretty Princess seemed out of place given his cultural background. My algorithms linked this mention to footage from the Bonnie Baroness, the cruise ship that went missing at sea. The cruise line was still investigating what happened, but I found multiple cell phone videos. One was stored in the Google Cloud of HappyFeet2012. The video was shot by a girl named Paulina and two older girls, Thalia and Wendy. They appeared to be acting out a scene from the ship's bow. Their presenter paused the footage to explain his reason for showing the following clip. They were laughing and joking around when they decided to get some lunch. Suddenly, they were knocked off balance. The shot jostled as towels and other personal items flew across the deck. The phone also fell but was caught by the owner's lanyard. People mumbled and called out to their friends as they regained their footing. Suddenly, a woman let out a scream.

"Paulina!" one of the girls clamored. She panned toward her sister and then to the water where she was pointing.

"Dolphins! They're jumping!" Paulina cried out in excitement.

"Happy Feet," corrected the voice of a woman off-camera, "Those are whales." As the massive ship rocked and bobbed again, you could hear commotion rise, sending the passengers off balance. The fin of the incubus broke the water's surface behind the pod of violently leaping whales near the ship, causing water displacement that made the colossal ship bobble from east to west like a rowboat.

"I'm going to TikTok -" A child's voice trailed off as the footage ended abruptly. The last clip was from Nic's phone of the entire annelation of the ship. After that clip, the lights in the room rose from a dim beam to full strength, illuminating Anton in complete seriousness. He took a deep breath and began.

"So, as you can see, things got calamitous really quick," he explained, "Furthermore, we have a boat anchor with weird DNA for you science geeks to check out. It was retrieved from the coast of the Philippines. The ship's remains were from a vessel with a history of illegal whaling. The metal was tested for whale DNA so they could take possession of the remains to hold the company liable. The Coast Guard's findings were inconclusive. Two days ago, we had it delivered here, which is where you two come in," he gestured to the Dr. Humboldts. "Well, plus that baby you already caught and were playing with at your school. It arrived here before you landed." Evelyn turned to Adem, blinking.

Turning to address the whole room, he asked, "Questions?" Everyone began talking at once.

"This is about the turd," Adem leaned over and whispered to his wife. She stood rigid in disbelief.

CHAPTER SIXTEEN

Caribou Coffee

AFTER ANSWERING a series of questions, Anton handed the interrogation over to Dru. Feeling like he'd already responded to the most essential questions, Anton slipped out the back door. He felt confident he could talk more tomorrow. Well, maybe he could, but only if he left now. Needing to unwind, he took Rukia for her walk while binge-watching Sword Art

Online, a classic animated series that pleased and entertained him more each time he watched.

As part of Anton's exceptionality, he could only tolerate high-energy groups of people for a limited period before growing emotionally overwhelmed, which often led to an inappropriate outburst or a shutdown. While walking the streets, he used a self-designed hybrid app on a pair of smart glasses. This device immersed him in an augmented reality simulation, allowing him to fully enjoy gaming, while an app designed to assist the visually impaired utilized cameras, a gyroscope, GPS, OLED displays, and vibrating sensors to navigate for him. In this way, he could escape by watching a show or playing a video game while traversing the city, oblivious to dangerous obstacles yet perfectly safe.

He ended up at Caribou Coffee, where he ordered a Nitro Turtle Mocha, a water cup, and a warm oatmeal cookie for his best girl. She took one sniff and turned her nose up at it, in no mood for a cookie when she could be napping in the condo. She was craving this perfect sliver of sunshine that hit the bed at this time of the afternoon. Hours passed, and he noticed storm clouds forming, followed by a wicked crack of thunder. Putting Rukia in her pup pack, he decided to jog home before the storm arrived. He realized she was missing her usual nap time. Anton worked in cycles of short, productive bursts that sometimes turned into binges of working for 18 to 36 hours, after which he would crash for 24 hours or more. He went missing for a few days, but was usually holed up in his lair. Michaels kept constant surveillance on him, which Anton wasn't fully aware of. Still, since he could no longer do anything legally wrong, a little digital supervision was a reasonable trade.

CHAPTER SEVENTEEN

Experiential

~ Four Days Later ~

AT 9:30 ON THURSDAY MORNING, Anton wandered into the office and into the newly assembled lab, tousle-haired and unkempt, followed dutifully by a drone carefully balancing cardboard drink carriers with piping hot coffee. Below that, on a modified appendage, hung a bag of muffins, bagels, and one quiche.

To everyone's alarm, he'd purchased something similar to what they would have ordered for themselves. Realizing that this kid not only had access to public records but probably knew their schedules for everything, they shrugged and decided not to worry about something so minor, given the gravity of what was happening in the world.

"Let's breakfast in the conference room. Brief me," Anton commanded casually as he walked past them toward the back of the lab. He pressed a tile on the east wall without explanation, which slid open to reveal a smooth obsidian hallway through a doorway. Dru held open the door directly across from the easement and nodded. He winked at her as the drone hovered in front of her. Cleverly, it took the door's weight off her and placed a small, triangular foot to keep the door propped open. He then extended a metallic, skeletal arm and, with its finger, skillfully sliced an opening into the bag, revealing Dru's pastry. She placed her hands on the side of the butler's canister-like head and kissed him.

"Thank you, FROLO," she murmured. Alex, leading the party with one eyebrow cocked, turned around to see if the others were noticing the groundbreaking technology on display. Evelyn cooed at the anthropomorphic relationship between Dru and the robot, and Adem muttered in disbelief as he entered the room.

"Humboldts, let's start with you." Anton directed as he bit into some exotic pastry and sipped his Dark Mocha Java. The team listened intently as they sipped their refreshments, the couple mentioning the scientific data that had corroborated Anton's theory.

"We suspect these animals have a territory based on the vicinity of the other megaladons," Evelyn explained, which was what they'd resorted to calling the animals for the time being. "When they are outside the range of others, they are stimulated to metamorphose."

"It's nature's way of distributing them across a large surface area." Adem clarified.

"We haven't agreed that these are Otodus megalodon." Evelyn interjected

"What else could they be?" Anton asked.

"Well, a species which we never imagined, obviously," TJ justified.

"—Or" Emmie interjected, "a megalodon could be a more complex organism than we previously knew, with the shark simply being one form in its life cycle. Whatever we call these animals, they seem to excrete a type of ink, similar to what modern jellyfish produce.

However, their excrement is unique because it contains copper and salt. When salt dissolves, the sodium and chloride anions are separated and surrounded by water molecules. Instead of dissolving, when this fecal compound disperses in saltwater, it forms a solid compound, copper chloride, which is denser and heavier than water. It clots into a large, membranous, cloudy mass that quickly sinks to the sea floor, removing the salt from the seawater. This development is going to make the ocean inhospitable for all ocean life," Emmie concluded. She and TJ had been working on this theory for the last two days.

TJ chimed in. "According to our simulations, this will likely have catastrophic environmental ramifications affecting the entire planet's ecosystem when this stercus binds with salt and makes it fall to the ocean floor. From here, it will expeditiously alter the upper levels of ocean water, beginning in the Sunlight Zone, the Twilight Zone, and finally, the Midnight Zone, while affecting the deepest levels. The Abyssoelagic and Hadal zones will be hypersaline, killing off all oceanic lifeforms.

Saltwater is denser than freshwater. This change in pressure is predicted to cause the freshwater to flow into rivers and lakes, triggering massive floods. With vegetation along the coasts drowning. This will likely generate an atmospheric cloud that could potentially trigger the mass extinction of all advanced species by reducing carbon dioxide."

Adem spoke up. "Furthermore, environmental statistical analysis predicts that this increase in freshwater levels from the oceans may ultimately lead to rising temperatures and melting of the polar ice caps. This phenomenon is likely to cause a die-off of the flora as root systems break down. Dust clouds, erosion of hills, and dirt storms that block sunlight could trigger the next ice age,"

"Additionally," Evelyn added, "This animal appears to be not only genetically related to modern immortal day jellyfish: Turritopsis dohrnii. The adult stage of this innovative creature grows, reaches adulthood, procreates: clones, and then, when she does not find enough nutrients, goes back into her amorphous stage."

Alex finally spoke up. "We could even go so far as to hypothesize that if this species has been trapped in that cavern for as long as we suspect, it could be as old as crude oil. It might have been responsible for the Great Dying, a world-ending event before Homo sapiens. We're talking about 2.6 million years ago," supplied Alex. Emmie nodded.

"Upon closer inspection," she said, "we have a running theory that the fossilized remains of the megalodon were just very small young adult specimens of this animal, which, through its life cycle, ultimately lives infinitely."

Evelyn jumped back in. "Stage one of its life cycle, the nymph stage, is an amorphous blob floating at the bottom of the ocean or, in this case, even beneath the crust, in a dormant state. Once disturbed, it moves to stage two, floating to the water's surface and forming a large blanket that feeds on plankton through osmosis and develops from stem cells in a multicellular plasma. As it nourishes itself, it begins to develop through the ingestion of plankton and the process of photosynthesis. It then advances into a churning tube and takes on different shapes. As it gains nourishment, it develops into a jellyfish and finally morphs into its adult form, stage three, which is a shark, or what was previously called the megalodon," explained Evelyn.

At this point, Anton took his heels off the conference table and sat upright. He pushed his glasses up onto his nose, took the last sip from his Caribou Java, grabbed the handles of his dog carrier bag, and got up.

"It's not a megalodon. It's an *Infinydon,*" he concluded. With this realization, he pressed a mirrored tile on the wall that popped open to reveal a mini-fridge where he kept a small stash of string cheese and dried apricots. Peeling off a tiny tendril of cheese and dangling it into his mouth, he said while chewing, "So, we're all going to die." He masticated while pondering. "Rukia," he called. His dog woke and followed him as he exited the room through another hidden door that no one else was yet aware of. "Dru, tell Michaels that I'm implementing the Forbidden Fruit Fortification," he said on his way out. Raising his hand as a final salute to her and the team, he said, "Later, Nerds," and left the group.

The room erupted into chaos as each team member proposed ideas on what to prioritize next. A helicopter took off from the landing pad to transport Anton and Rukia to the master treehouse he built, waiting at the Klamath River Overlook in the Redwood Forest. His contract specified that he and his companion would be taken to his safe house after the researchers had been debriefed.

CHAPTER EIGHTEEN

Abandon Camp

Delsin hurriedly packed up his campsite, forced to leave behind most of the belongings he'd accumulated over the summer. When he'd gotten home earlier, he'd found a written warning from the sheriff's office, giving him a short time to vacate before the landowner returned with law enforcement and issued an order to arrest him for trespassing and littering.

The notice read:

§11-22-123. Vagrancy: Universal Citation: 11 OK Stat § 11-22-123 (2014)

The municipal governing body may provide by ordinance for the arrest, fine, and imprisonment of vagrants.

Dickwads, he thought, packing his necessities into his rucksack. This bag was a lucky find early on his journey. It was lightweight yet roomy, breathable, and water-resistant. There were days when it was his only shelter from downpour. He made his way back to the road, drawn toward the city. There were undoubtedly more resources there. It was just so damn loud. After some deliberation, he decided to stay in Oklahoma City until he grew overwhelmed. To the city, it was.

Three days later, Delsin was set up on MacArthur Boulevard and Nineteenth Street in the Windsor Forest neighborhood. He had gotten settled before dawn, put out his coffee can, and quickly drifted into a deep reverie. He started to wake up around 9:00 a.m. to find a strange group of smiling faces sitting cross-legged nearby. Two doors down, a woman sitting gracefully at a bistro set outside Cosmos Coffee noticed him stirring and hurried over with a cold water bottle and a fresh scone wrapped in tissue paper of seraphim blue.

"He's back!" she murmured to her companion as she left her post and moved to his aid. He pulled away from her fragile hands when he saw a middle-aged blonde woman nearly touching his face. Defensively, he flung his right arm out, knocking the crumbling pastry to the sidewalk, still oblivious to his surroundings. She yipped in alarm while tumbling back, trying to speak over his unease, telling him she meant no harm. Resting back on his left forearm, he blinked, confused by his enthusiastic audience.

"Delsin?" a silver-haired man called in a calming tone, approaching. "We're all wondering if you're okay." He explained as he crouched near the man from a safe distance. "My name is Gideon Richards. I'm with a small group that's growing quickly," he gestured widely with his arms, "a group of men and women eager to hear your divine message." Gideon paused as Delsin looked around at the group and then back at him. Delsin found his feet and took a few steps back. "Don't be alarmed. The group and I want to help you.

We've seen videos of your... speeches online, and we want to learn more about your celestial knowledge." Not entirely sure which videos this man meant, Delsin looked from face to face, all smiling joyfully.

He couldn't understand what they found so pleasing since his message was not one of happiness. It was a dark message about how Mother Earth is threatening to eliminate us to reclaim her power. She plans to recycle mankind, the most destructive species, so she and her other inhabitants can survive. Unable to understand what this group was really about and troubled by their jubilant appearance, he ran. He ran away from them all. He fled, hiding, hoping they would never find him.

Delsin walked all day erratically without

pausing to find sustenance and, only after sundown, ran out of gas near the doors of a nondescript shelter that he hoped might be just as covert as any place. He entered and was offered a shower and a cot, but no food. Freshly bathed, his empty stomach turned in knots with famine. He ignored that familiar sensation, pulling his clean but tangled hair off his forehead as he reclined onto the too-short cot, attempting to quiet his mind for the night when Gideon walked into the dimly lit room. The man had resources and had been surveilling him. He had been notified the moment Delsin was admitted.

This time, he approached the young man more cautiously. Delsin immediately sat up and stood stiffly at attention, the muscles in his neck visibly throbbing as his blood pressure started to climb. Gideon held his hands palm out to signal peace while he pulled up a chair and moved it close to the cot, leaving a respectful amount of space. He asked Delsin to sit in the chair next to him, but he refused.

"It's okay," he began amicably. "I'm not here to offer you anything you don't willfully choose to accept, Son. I want nothing from you but to better understand your message," he paused, but Delsin did not say anything in response. He continued, "Videos of you have been popping up.

One video went viral. Then other people started recording you and posting to an account that a woman created in your honor after you spoke of catastrophic events that had not yet appeared on the news, which came to light afterward. This helped us understand that the information you give is truly inspired. Your mother and sister saw them and have been corresponding with the group, hoping to establish contact with you. The coalition is based in New York. We have an apartment for you where you can meditate in peace. We will provide for you, meeting your physical needs, so you can focus on divination in the hope that we can understand and make amends with your Mother Earth."

He paused, giving Delsin a few minutes to process this information. He spent a few minutes in consideration, but upon second thought, tensed visibly in suspicion.

"Listen, Son, a Greenbucks account was opened for you so the public could donate to support your care, allowing you to focus on your abilities in the safety of a home without fear of judgment or danger. It already has $1.2 million in it that legally belongs to you. The woman who tried to feed you breakfast is the trustee, but she can only pay your taxes, not withdraw any funds." He paused, trying to read the stoic young man but getting nothing. "Let me at least buy you dinner so we can talk. I know you haven't eaten today." At that suggestion, his stomach let out a loud rumble, and Delsin felt like listening to this guy was at least worth a meal. He would eat as much as possible, and Delsin figured he could kick his ass if he got pervy. This guy was old, he thought, like 60. He grabbed his pack, stood up, slipped his feet into his unlaced boots, and shrugged in acceptance of the offer of a hot meal. Gideon sat waiting for verbal acknowledgment, so there was no room for misunderstanding.

"Well, Old man, let's go."

CHAPTER NINETEEN

Dirty Magazine

THE AFTERNOON COURTYARD was sunlit by the shade trees of Holy Trinity Parish. Playful sunbeams flickered on the calm water of the large fountain. The melodies of birds and the rush of wind through the treetops muffled the city's noise pollution, turning it into gentle white noise. For that reason and many others, Father Johnson loved it here. He sat by the fountain, finally opening up about what he'd been going through, while Father Bromley pruned the rose bushes, appearing uninterested as he clipped the hedges. Knowing that his friend was nearly deaf, he felt comfortable speaking his mind without fear of judgment. No matter what was said, Father Bromley would nod and smile in understanding.

"This thing is enormous. She grows bigger every day. I can tell because she eats anything, and here's the strangest part: she seems aware of her digestion. When she defecates, it's like she's passing an eighteen-wheeler—so dense and heavy, but only after exposure to water. The stool turbulently absorbs the salt in the water for a few minutes. When it reaches a certain saturation point, the entire mess sinks like a boulder, and I can feel the water in my own lungs changing, becoming less alkaline. But it doesn't alarm her; she's built for this. All those other sea creatures aren't. They're flailing around, dying. They look like little astronauts who lost their helmets. They're fading, and she's just watching them struggle. She cares about their loss, which saddens her, but she knows it's all for the greater good. But you know who she's really after, man! Do you know how people say that Great Whites are man-eaters? They're not. Sometimes a person just gets in their way. This lady is looking for humans to kill. She is driven by a mission to eradicate us. It's pretty frightening, but we're safe as long as we stay out of the water. It makes me nervous that we live on the coast. I won't go swimming anytime soon.

A loud rap from an upstairs window grabbed their attention.

"Father Johnson," the Monsignor called in admonition from his office window. "Don't you have an appointment to attend?" he hollered from the third-story window, glancing at his watch. His disapproval of his parishioner openly sharing his supernatural experience with his peers was clear. He seemed to regret giving Johnson so much time off, now busying himself with idle chitchat and exploring mystical theories about what might be happening to him.

"Yes, Monsignor. I was just about to leave," he said, waving one hand over his head. He started making dramatic gestures as if to gather himself to go, but when he saw the shadow leave the windowsill, he settled back onto the fountain.

"So, do you think this monster is God?" Father Bromley asked him outright.

"I couldn't say. It feels distinctly female. Could the Almighty be a woman after all?" The two men chuckled at such a silly idea. Driven by his conscience for indulging in this innocent yet thrilling guilty pleasure of gossip, Chris looked out the window and saw the Monsignor glaring down at him with his arms crossed over a protruding belly, especially noticeable from that angle. Hiding his snickers at being caught challenging his superior, he nervously hopped up, acting more like a mischievous student than a middle-aged man. He was amused at being caught and pointed at his peer to shift the blame. Father Bromley turned to see their critic at the window, glaring sternly; Chris genuinely started to head out while his companion pointed back at him, shaking his head in disagreement, unwilling to share the blame.

Hours later, Chris sat naked except for a gown, his cheeks pressed uncomfortably against a hospital cot, waiting for his results. He fiddled with his nails and looked around the room for the hundredth time. Over the past ninety minutes, he had his blood drawn for a complete blood panel, received a tracer injection, been instructed to empty his bladder and urinate into a plastic cup, and lay down in a coffin-like PET-CT bed. It was nerve-wracking to listen to buzzing and clicking sounds and to stay still for over an hour, plagued by unsettling thoughts.

"It's definitely a tumor. I read about it on WebMD, which would explain the headaches and his loss of sanity," he grumbled aloud.

When no one argued otherwise, he decided to lie back and try to relax. As he was dozing off, an annoyingly pretty nurse came in just long enough to make him sit up. She smiled and set down a Dixie cup of tap water so he could rehydrate. He grabbed the cup and sat back down. Swallowing the metallic-tasting liquid, he scrunched his nose, crumpled the cup, and tossed it toward the wastebasket. He missed. Staring at the cup lying on the floor, it seemed to mock him. He peered closer, noticing some hair and fuzz just behind the counter's overhang. *Nasty,* he thought, shivering a little. *I've never been an athlete,* he acknowledged sadly. Contemplating how many baskets he'd made in his life? None? Had he really made zero baskets in his whole life?

"That seems a shame," he mumbled. "Maybe

I should make just one before this cancer puts me in my grave." He announced to the medical mannequin, which was modeling the circulatory system in the corner. He scooted off the table, his bare feet slapping on the cold tiled floor. He clumsily reached down over his belly and teetered before grabbing the cup. He took five steps back to the door and raised both hands, ready to shoot. Tongue sticking out in concentration, he flicked his wrist and made the shot with a tiny hop. It fell eighteen inches short of the basket. He glared at the cup as if wondering why it was so awkward. Shrugging, he shuffled forward and, with his foot, pushed the trash out of sight, knocking his big toe against the counter, wincing. Growling some forbidden four-letter words, he climbed back onto the examining table.

Having already studied the charts of the human nasal system on the wall thoroughly, he turned to thumbing through a Cosmo magazine that promised to teach him ten tips for having a Hot Girl Summer. *What does that mean?* he wondered? Disappointed this was the only entertainment available while waiting for the doctor to return, he opened to the first glossy page to see a pale-skinned girl with an unnatural pout in a back-breaking pose. She was wearing stilettos, a long skirt, and a… *bra? Was this young lady in underwear?* he questioned. He could actually see her… *nipples! No! Surely not,* he reasoned. Holding the image closer, he squinted more carefully, his palms sweaty, to examine the photograph. They appeared peachy, he observed. His eyebrows raised in disbelief.

"I can't look at this!" He proclaimed loudly,

slamming the magazine shut and trying to focus on holy things. He thought about the church's regal leaders, then the Gospels, and passages mentioning Esther and Mary Magdalene. *Were their breasts like budding roses, too?* His mind raced, thoughts swirling. His hospital gown began to reveal a small but proud tent. He anxiously tugged at the fabric and imagined how hot hell might be after this tumor ended his life. But then again, there were immoral women there. *Ugh! YES! Demon temptresses. Not attractive! STOP!* he told himself as he waited for the doctor to return and read his results.

A sharp knock on the door interrupted his hedonistic introspection. He sat soberly, listening to the Indian doctor trying to decipher his meaning through his accent. His eyes refocused on the waxy litter of the Dixie cup as the doctor explained all the typical results of his blood tests and PET scan.

We did not notice any bright spots indicating higher levels of chemical activity that could provide insight into how your tissues and organs function. A specialist will review your exam and mail you the detailed report, but I told Monsignor Belli that I would share my preliminary opinion today. You are fine except for a stress-related sleep disorder. Here's a prescription for Somnafil. This will sedate you so you can rest. I've already called the Monsignor and informed him that you need your sabbatical extended by two weeks so you can rest and recover. Do you have any questions?" the doctor asked.

"I guess not," the baffled man uttered, shifting his weight to dismount the table, pick up that contemptuous cup, and get dressed.

CHAPTER TWENTY

Stratagem

THE TEAM WAS SETTLING into the conference room with deli sandwiches during another late-night think tank session before breaking to rest.

"You start." Dru pointed at Evelyn to kick off the meeting.

"Oh!" Evelyn covered her mouth, relishing a delicious mouthful. Holding a finger up, she pantomimed the chewing motion, asking for a moment.

"Well, I love deli," she said with a mouthful. "Okay. So, other than mass destruction and all that mayhem," she began, dabbing the dressing from the corner of her mouth, "we predict significant changes globally. Already, regions worldwide are experiencing increased temperatures, resulting in glacial retreat, reduced snow cover, and shrinking ice sheets. Consequently, the oceans are warming, becoming more acidic, and rising, which leads to increased flooding. Marine life is dying off in huge numbers.

Dru put her drink down and added, "We can expect this activity to lead to more severe weather events: hurricanes, tsunamis, torrential rains, hail, snow, flooding, tornadoes, dust storms, earthquakes, and in extreme cases, volcanic eruptions," Dru said. Alex took a sip of his drink and set it down, refocusing their attention on more immediate issues.

Let's concentrate on what's happening now instead of guessing about what might happen later. Besides the monster killing people, the biggest concern is the damage it causes to the ocean. This change is destroying all the wildlife. Once the marine life is gone, what's next? When the entire chemical composition of the ocean is altered, what will happen to our planet? And what is that thing under the water, terrorizing and devouring everything in its way? Whatever it is, it's primal, ancient, and driven by instinct." FROLO rolled in. Emmie swallowed her bite and chimed in.

"We can safely assume that temperatures will keep rising because of the greenhouse effect," Emmie elaborated, thinking aloud. Alex was surprised.

"Global Warming?" He asked. "That's the danger for us on land? Isn't that supposed to occur over hundreds or thousands of years, after we're all dead?" Alex asked with a mouthful. Dru countered.

"We've been basing those estimates on our current ecosystem and environmental conditions. Our biosphere has just shifted. A new, powerful predator is changing things faster than any other species in recorded history," Dru said. After sharing her thought, she dipped her sandwich deep into the hot au jus and took a big bite, broth dripping carelessly as if their species weren't in mortal danger. FROLO moved forward, dabbing at her chin with a napkin using one skeletal arm. TJ jumped in.

"The idea that this species might have been

responsible for the last mass extinction is disturbing," Alex joined in.

"Also, did we decide this thing is a Carcharocles megalodon?" Adem asked the group, "Based on fossilized records cross-referenced with DNA."

"An Infinydon." Evelyn redressed.

"Where did that come from?" TJ asked.

"That's what Anton named her," Evelyn explained. "It's a megalodon that lives infinitely." Adem went on.

"Fossils of this animal in its juvenile stage were identified as the Carcharocles megalodon, but this creature is not what we believed the meg to be. The largest fossils we've found measured 60 feet long, which is three times the size of a great white," Adem answered.

“The animal we are chasing now has already outgrown the Balaenoptera musculus, the modern blue whale, which has been recorded at over 100 feet or 30 meters in length. This thing might be twice that size," Evelyn added.

Dru said, “Megalodon was believed to have gone extinct 20 million years ago in the Pliocene Epoch. This thing lives forever,” Dru pointed out.

Alex held up a hand. “If that’s the case, how do we have fossilized remains?” Alex contested, pointing out a glaring flaw in the argument.

"We talked about that yesterday. The only theory we have right now is that they are vulnerable in their young adult form and can be killed if threatened during that time, but at the size she is now, I fear that window has closed," Emmie explained.

"Do we all agree?" Alex asked the group. "On the name Carcharocles infinydon?"

"Aye!" Each nodded, raising their right hand and mumbling in agreement while chewing.

"Most importantly, how do we stop it?" Emmie asked, causing the room to fall silent as each member thought quietly without any solid ideas.

"Guys! We need a plan!" TJ insisted.

CHAPTER TWENTY-ONE

Penthouse

DELSIN CLOSED HIS LAPTOP on the sofa of his penthouse in the Convivium Complex on 86th Street in New York City. He had just finished another webcam interview, where he was asked about the sudden glacial retreat and the shrinking ice sheets. Delsin wasn't there in person because he had stopped traveling. He said every second of his time was precious, and he often felt debilitated, with his visions becoming more frequent and intense these weeks. He dialed his phone.

"Del, you were great! I believe we conveyed our message effectively. People are getting it. They are changing! How do you feel?" Gideon asked supportively.

"No more interviews," Delsin said. "It's too late for change. I'll keep streaming my visions for the followers, but no more interviews." He paused, listening to silence on the other end, Gideon playing his hand by not speaking. "People don't believe me, and besides, we're out of time," Delsin said gloomily. His eyes drifted to the rising water level of the ocean through the high-rise window, then to the bedroom doors behind which his mother and sister were peacefully resting. "All the beaches are underwater, even at low tide, and we've had more tidal waves now as we approach the full moon. Man has lived. We abused our power. Our time has come to an end. I'm ready." The line remained silent.

"Well, that's dark," Gideon finally said. "What can we do?" he asked, concern in his voice.

"We can give thanks for our time, express gratitude. We can meditate on our next destination, but we can no longer stay here," the young man explained. Gideon held his breath on the other end of the line. "That's what I've been telling you, people." Again, Gideon was at a loss for words.

"What encouragement can you offer a man in touch with the universe who's just been given the memo that our extinction was booked and scheduled?" he asked. Delsin failed to respond. "How much time?" he asked, thoughtfully digesting the gravity of this new reality.

"Weeks. Days, maybe." Delsin guessed. "I don't know, Man."

"Well, your rent is paid up until the end of this year. The place is all yours. Do you need anything else from me?" Gideon asked as a last service of duty. "I'm going to spend time with my daughters and grandkids. And soon enough, maybe I'll be with my late wife again." His voice grew thick with emotion. Taking a deep breath, he said thoughtfully, "Well, I guess we all will," he inserted, defeated, attempting to sound half as brave as the young warrior. "Well, call if you want to, but I'll not schedule anything more. I'm going to stop working and spend time living," he explained. "You know, I've always wanted to touch a snake, a giant python," Delsin raised one eyebrow at this confession. "And try French wine and soak in a hot tub naked. I think I'll do those things too," Gideon confessed.

Delsin smiled at this. "You do that." With that, the conversation was over. Delsin looked at the coalition secretary's notification on his laptop that a priest wanted to meet with him.

"No more appointments." Delsin wrote back and changed his email settings to Do Not Disturb. He turned on the television and immediately muted it to silence the shrieking coming from the news showing a montage of exotic resorts deep underwater. There were other stories of freak storms, volcanic eruptions, and earthquakes. Then came footage of the recovered wreckage of the cruise liner, and meteorologists excitedly predicted a crisis while discouraging panic.

Shaking his head in sorrow, he turned off the power and stood at the window, watching the waves crash against the buildings that were once just a few blocks from the beach. He reflected on how hard his time on this earth had been but expressed gratitude to the Great Spirits for his gift. He apologized for his past actions while trying to quiet their voices. He was thankful to be sober. Since being placed in a safe place where he could rest, get regular nourishment, and allow his visions to happen whenever needed, he no longer experienced such debilitating headaches. He watched the surf batter the abandoned beachfront properties from his window. After a few minutes, he sensed that another episode was approaching. He logged onto the YouTube channel the group had designated and set his computer to live stream. He took a long drink of water and sat on the floor in front of his couch for support to ensure he wouldn't fall. He did his best to relax, propping two pillows behind his head, leaning back, and letting nature take its course.

Within sixty seconds, 32,804 viewers were online, hundreds of whom were typing furiously in the chat to him and each other.

"Marry me, Buck!" -hawtToddy22

"Were gonna dye." -Freddy$unds

“Hi, Sara! U there?” -FaithHope&Love

“I wuz 1st” -CandieKane

“It’s 2 funcking hot out here! Wtf?” DrHungover

“What u going to say 2day, Delsun?” -Shaggydawg

“I’m going to go surfing today, dare me” Drummerdude

“Git me pregs, segsy.” SunnyDeed

“This is happening because of the polar icecaps are melting” Flowrgurl.

"No itsbecuz of evil people going to hail." -JohnieBeegood

The nonsensical chat feed continued, moving so quickly that no one could keep up with it. There were people dropping money and proclamations of love and hate for Delsin. Some were making predictions about today's session, but few listened as his head rose and he began to recite the ancient wisdom on the Great Spirits. Hearing his moans and cries crescendo, his mother emerged from her room and saw that he was safe, just in cogitation. Taking care not to walk into the camera frame, she sat across from him on the other couch, tucking her long ebony hair behind her ear, watching her son, the miracle, the seer, the one who knows things.

Clutching the talisman around her neck, she said her own kind of prayer in thanks for the sacred vessel born of her womb. She sat back, legs folded beneath her, watching her baby boy contort with distress as divine messages were passed from his body and out of his mouth. She wept as she listened to the message he delivered.

CHAPTER TWENTY-TWO

Steak Tartare

DRU ENTERED THE LAB mid-morning with FROLO in tow, delivering coffee. Having worked until three the previous morning, they all agreed not to report to work until nine, rest being essential for such revolutionary intellectual exploration. Evelyn, Emmie, and TJ worked with Anton remotely from his central processing unit, running strategy simulations. Alex was off examining water samples under the microscope.

"Yes!" TJ exclaimed at the latest replication.

"Thank you," Emmie said graciously, turning at the scent of steaming coffee, smirking with self-satisfaction. Evelyn reached out behind her without taking her eyes off the screen.

"This could work!" she exclaimed. "This might actually work!"

"What could?" Adem asked, just reporting for duty, scrubbing his hands over his face and rubbing sleep away.

"Well, good morning, Sleeping Beauty," she greeted him, jumping up excitedly and tiptoeing to give him a quick kiss on his scratchy chin. He sweetly patted the top of her head to acknowledge her affection while still letting her know he needed a few more minutes to reciprocate. With a polite nod, he snatched his chai from the drink carrier, the potent aroma of ginger and cinnamon wafting, and mounted the nearest stool. He took a cautious sip, gauging the heat. Unscathed, he took a deeper pull while admiring his wife across the lab, appreciating how extraordinary she was, even when a little disheveled from sleep deprivation: a lopsided bun, bare skin with makeup, casual jeans, and tennis shoes.

Leaning toward her, Adem left a quick kiss on her temple before moving to her side and, in a sleep-rasped voice, asked, "Well, what have I missed?"

"Just watch!" she nudged her shoulder into his chest. At the sound of this excitement, compelled by the power of caffeine, Alex got up from his microscope. Cup in one hand, high-fiving Dru with his free hand and fist-bumping FROLO, he strode over to see what was happening on the monitor. They all watched in suspense as the animation progressed with the beacon signal luring the shark. Just as the beast consumed the target, BOOM! She was injected with a cryogenic solution that would turn her into ice.

"According to your Doppler readings of her biorhythms, this will draw her into the snare," Dru asked Evelyn, "As long as we can properly emit this frequency?"

FROLO made a short series of beeps, a

whistling sound, and then, in a robotic voice not unlike Bumblebee's, said, "We'll need some serious darts to inject that massive bitch!" Everyone on the team turned and looked at the cybernetic organism.

"You can talk?" Adem asked incredulously. They all broke into hysterical gaiety; their joy prompted by this remarkable finding, but hearing the robot say something so unanticipated had them all enlivened with celebration!

Alex announced, "We've been living in this lab for seventeen days. There are so many amazing restaurants in DC. Let's go to lunch and celebrate while there is still civilized life left on Earth. We'll, come back afterward and work on an implementation plan, after a long lunch."

"It will be like a Last Supper," Dru lamented morosely.

"Dark," said TJ.

"Here, here," the team said, raising their disposable cups all but Evelyn.

"But, should we really quit now?" she wondered aloud.

"We're not quitting, just taking a short break: two hours," Adem clarified in a coddling tone. "I'll set a timer," he promised. She tried batting him away as he put his arms around her to guide her outside the lab. She continued to resist weakly, naturally tempted by the idea of tantalizing cuisine. He turned to face her, putting his rough hands on her cheeks.

"Sweet Pea, everything will be fine," he

assured her, hugging her tightly and kissing her pursed lips, cutting off any further argument. Wrapped in his arms, she went limp. She started giggling. Then fell silent. Arms wrapped around his neck, she asked, quivering into his ear.

"Make love to me tonight?"

"You can bet your life on it," he answered back. She smiled tenderly and then grimaced, considering the figure of speech in which one bets on another's life, dire times as these were. He cunningly set his timer for three hours while FROLO ordered a car, saying he was going to slam a tequila shot.

"You drink?" TJ asked the droid, now in even greater disbelief.

"I'll take that shaken, not stirred," FROLO responded in the distinguished voice of James

Bond. The Brain Trust all erupted into laughter as they headed off for some much-needed downtime. To travel together, FROLO ordered a limo where the festivities began. The group settled on Brasserie Liberté. While being chauffeured, they sipped champagne and relaxed, letting go of their worries. Upon arrival, the group was led into a private room with numerous attendants.

They began jubilantly by sharing hors d'oeuvres from each other's plates as a family would. They sipped French onion soup gratinée, nibbled petite salad with green peppercorn sauce, on steak tartare, ornate quail eggs, escargots sauvages de Bourgogne, and warm baguettes while sipping complimentary spirits. Agreeing to discuss anything but work, they unwound as the wait staff continued to bring out tantalizing treasures. They sampled sumptuous dishes drowned liberally in savory sauces and partook of ambrosial wines as the hours passed. As the afternoon waned, they sipped flavorful sparkling drinks accompanied by mouthwatering smoked Gruyère, Mornay with brandade croquettes, macaroni au gratin, and burrata with toasted hazelnuts, pomegranate seeds, orange segments, and a light basil oil.

Somewhat inebriated, they recounted their interpretations of each other in those first few days, chortling at FROLO's remarkable impersonations that pegged them each impeccably. They were amused by his uncanny ability to intuitively replay key moments of their interactions, capturing their individuality. It was bizarre to observe this automaton performing his parodies in such a humorous manner.

It made Evelyn retrospectively consider the implications of the machine's survival through this event, while humans became extinct, and machines potentially became the next overseers of the world. Shaking her head, she dismissed the idea with the concluding hope that, in that case, they were more considerate of nature instead of exploitation and dominant. The afternoon passed, and as Dru picked off the last crumbs of Alex's cheesecake from his plate, Adem pushed back his chair and proposed a toast. Evelyn held up her glass and tapped, making three brilliant chimes. The party all fell to attention, all eyes on the tall, strapping scientist.

A month ago, I never would have imagined myself dining in such an elegant place with such a distinguished group, all of whom were planning to save the world. No matter what lies ahead, I will cherish this moment we shared and the love I have for my wife." Everyone nodded in agreement. "To the turds," Adem announced.

"To the turds," everyone repeated in triumph, laughing, clinking glasses, hugging, and making merry.

Suddenly, Michaels pushed through the door with the squat yet fastidious restaurant manager trailing after him, exhibiting an argument contrary to his actions, that he had received presidential orders stating this party was not to be disturbed. Noting his dampened brow and sour expression, the party grew quiet. FROLO stood and, with one metallic skeletal hand at his temple, stood rigidly as if in respectful salute.

"FROLO," greeted the commander with a nod but no return salute. "We have-" He was cut off by the droid in Robin Williams' voice.

"Good morning, Vietnam! This is not a test. This is rock and roll. Time to rock it from the delta to the DMZ!" FROLO belted out over a loudspeaker, mocking Michael's militaristic disposition. The entire room lost it, sending the team and serving staff into uproarious laughter that had them all howling until their faces were tear-streaked. Even Michaels had to smile at his mischievous impersonation.

"If you've all finished your brunch…" he said, tapping his crystal-faced watch. The group began shuffling around, wiping their faces on soft linen and pushing their plates away, mildly to moderately inebriated. They simultaneously reached behind them and under the tables for their bags as the wait staff hurriedly delivered overcoats and sweaters. As they left their cozy alcove, they could see through the glass front of the dining room that the weather had taken a nasty turn, and another menacing storm was blowing in, causing the trees to bend and bow in the horizontal rain. A darkness fell over the group that sobered them up during the somber ride back to the lab.

CHAPTER TWENTY-THREE

Exodus

FATHER JOHNSON was clearly skeptical of the doctor's clean bill of health. Despite the story he'd been raised to believe, he'd started questioning whether he genuinely had a direct connection to God. *Were these visions the insight he was subconsciously seeking? No. Definitely not. Was this the work of the devil,* he wondered? *Maybe. Perhaps demons were invited because of his lack of faith;* he grimaced, sickened. He sat in his sweat-soaked bathrobe, no longer enjoying his days off. Without his usual routine, his days were filled with restless, unproductive sleep, and his nights proved anything but peaceful. He increasingly experienced intense visions.

His suffering grew more surreal each time he witnessed the destruction of the known world. He'd observed each stage of this creature's development. In her primitive form, he clearly sensed a consciousness. Although ancient, this was not her first life cycle on our planet. She'd wiped out civilizations before—advanced societies of other top predators that had run their course. He clicked his tongue, which felt as dry as cotton, and sipped from the glass of water on his nightstand before noticing the tiny moth drowned in it.

He coughed, smacking his lips, now tasting the dust of wing scale in his mouth. Gruffly, he toasted a bagel and propped up his phone to check his YouTube notifications. He'd recently subscribed to several channels that covered the catastrophe in various ways.

The first time he saw an event reported that he had telepathically witnessed, he was dazed by the implications, confirming his growing suspicion that this was very real. He flushed the sleeping pills, suspecting they weren't stopping the night terrors, just erasing his memory of them when he woke up. He thought that his experience might be important.

Mind whirling, with one ear cocked toward the video describing the rising predictions, he snatched his bagel from the toaster. Tossing it from one toasty finger to another, crumbs fell beneath brittle, shuffling feet with yellowed toenails. Having traveled the four steps from the countertop to the table-for-one, he plopped his modest meal onto the surface, crumbs scattering in all directions. Tongue sticking out in concentration, he topped his pastry with an excess of blueberry cream cheese while staring fixedly at his phone. With one chubby finger, he clicked on the notification that Fiero's World News had posted in their Friday episode.

He clicked on it and started listening to a blurb about a man named Delsin Buck. This man, Chris distinguished, seemed to be suffering a similar ailment. Against his churning gut, he jotted down the email address in the margin of his leather-bound Bible, in the book of

Jeremiah, near where God says that He has plans for us to prosper and not to harm, and not to give up hope for a future. *Is that until we mess up?* Christopher wondered, considering the last Exodus: the flood. Pushing through his hesitation, he composed a message to the young man, telling him everything he knew and pleading for a meeting. His hope was to confirm, even from a lunatic, that he wasn't crazy.

CHAPTER TWENTY-FOUR

Modest Measure

ALEX ENJOYED THE SWEET AROMA of the steaming pecan roast delivered by Dru, but cast half-hearted looks of annoyance at the bedroom eyes Evelyn was giving Adem from across the lab.

"Get a room, you two!" he finally said. TJ looked up from his simulation, smiling and exchanging subtle eye contact with Emmie.

"I think it's sweet," Emmie said, smirking shyly. Dru piped up, her youthful eyebrows raised at her elders.

"We all need to find joy wherever we can. We don't know what the next month might bring.

"Month? Try about seventeen days," TJ said.

"Seventeen days until what?" Alex queried.

TJ answered, "My system's analysis of the oceanic soil and water samples we received indicates that we have less than three weeks before irreversible changes happen on our planet." he paused, looking at each of them. "A mass extinction event, not just of people, but all advanced lifeforms," explained TJ.

"Um…Everybody, come see this!" Dru called from the large workstation at the far end of the room. Anton just sent this footage from his safe house in the trees. Check out this broadcast from the Voyage Data Recorder on the Bonnie Baroness.

"Who?" Alex asked.

"That ship that went missing," Adem reminded him. The group gathered, sitting on stools. Emmie perched on the countertop, TJ standing close enough to smell her coconut shampoo. For a moment, he studied her features as she watched the screen, long lashes casting shadows on her cheeks. Her cheeks flushed slightly as she quietly tucked her loose hair.

behind her ear, he realized he was caught and averted his gaze. Turning to the monitor, he gawked as the behemoth beached herself on the deck of the cruise ship.

Evelyn stood. “Pause right there. Look at that. She has longer dorsal fins than a modern-day blue shark." This rare footage of her allowed them to examine her anatomy in great detail.

“Yeah. Huge,” agreed Alex.

“Yes, but look here,” said Adem, approaching the monitor. "Her fins are large compared to a Great White of similar size. She’s actually shaped a bit more like a blue shark.”

“What happened to her face?” TJ asked, noting scarring.

“There’s that too,” Evelyn recorded.

"Why is she so aggressive? Can you determine its gender?" he asked curiously.

Evelyn responded. "I'm not seeing a pair of claspers, which are male indicators in many modern sharks," Evelyn examined. "More importantly, can she buccal pump? If so, she won't need to be submerged to breathe."

"I'm guessing so," Adem observed, "because she's already been out of the water for five minutes and doesn't seem compromised."

"She's calculating," Emmie said nervously, studying her.

Evelyn puzzled, examining the dermal denticles, observing the subtle color change. "A shark's skin, or shagreen, resembles a cat's tongue—rough on one side but smooth on the other—helping them glide through the water," she told them.

"Would that be hydrodynamics?" Alex asked.

"Precisely," Evelyn replied absentmindedly, still wondering whether those scales were shifting tone.

As the recording played out the catastrophe, the team members took turns covering their mouths and muttering obscenities. When the entire beast was captured on screen, Dru paused the image, and simulated measurements were taken.

"The infinydon is estimated to be three hundred fifty-six feet long," Dru announced.

“That can’t be right!” TJ said.

“That measurement is a modest estimate, overcompensating for perspective,” Dru responded. The rest of the footage was watched in silence, with the group huddled together in solidarity. Paralyzed, Evelyn was struck by the gravity of what they were facing.

Adem was the first to speak. “I need a blueprint of her anatomy, the best we can concoct, to engineer an ambush.”

“We need to trap her," Evelyn said. "I hoped that lifting her out of the water would allow nature to handle it, but she doesn’t seem bothered being on land. I doubt she could stay beached for long due to her weight. It’s going to be difficult to control her."

"She has to die," Alex said, taking the last sip of his coffee and tossing the cup into the trash in a defiant act of finality.

Dru returned from the bathroom with her kinky curls in a fresh ponytail and said, "Take a short recess. Conference Room in Ten. Team, we're going to have to kill this primordial bitch!"

After a few minutes of regrouping, the group trickled in and saw the list of facts compiled.

Adem started by saying, "For the record, as a scientist, it seems ethical to collect her and study her at least for a while."

"But," Evelyn interrupted, "we've established beyond a reasonable doubt that she's too dangerous, and we don't have the resources to house or care for an animal as powerful, dangerous, and massive as she."

"So, we agree on euthanasia?" TJ asked.

"Well, it'll be her or us," Emmie said.

Alex broke in, "Let's try to think of this objectively. Is it possible that we have lived out our reign as the dominant lifeform on this planet?"

"We've been terrible stewards of the planet the last few centuries," Evelyn resolved.

TJ added, "Objectively, we've been the worst keepers the planet's ever had. We're the only species in known history to waste without restraint, kill each other carelessly, damage our environment to the point of climate change, and cause the extinction of countless plant and animal species." -TJ agreed.

"What are you guys saying? Maybe our time as a species is over?" Emmie asked incredulously.

Adem emphasized, "We should approach the situation and actions with scientific rigor and careful thought. We need to make an effort to detach emotionally and analyze potential solutions systematically and mathematically.

Evelyn nodded. "If we win this war, what are the chances that mankind will survive the foreseeable future given our destructive habits?" she contemplated.

Dru informed them, "These numbers have already been calculated, and it's been established that Earth's destruction is imminent. There is another team researching the colonization of other planets. We're preparing for our planet's demise as a direct result of human behavior. That was in the works, but has been escalated. It seems we're out of time," Dru remarked.

Disturbed, Alex said, "So… if we beat this thing and live, we're still going to die? Not only are we doomed, but likely most other lifeforms on this planet as well?" Alex asked.

"Is it not too late to change?" Adem debated, really not liking the turn of this conversation.

"Our behavioral change would have to be radical," Emmie rationalized. "We've overpopulated the planet. We'd need to alter our way of life completely, returning to living off the land in harmony with nature and learning to stop taking more than the earth willingly gives.

We'd have to give up fossil fuels and rely solely on renewable energy, end mass agriculture and the use of chemicals and pesticides. Of course, we would also have to eliminate pollution and unnecessary waste."

Due shook her head, "Mankind would never agree if left up to them. People would rather stick their heads in the sand and ignore the situation. If it's not directly affecting them today, they are going to give up comfort and make the change."

Adem affirmed, "Tony Robbins said it best when he said that change happens when the pain of staying the same is greater than the pain of change. The pain of what is about to happen is too great for most people even to fathom.

Alex argued, "It's true, but from a biological perspective, lying down before our competitor goes against our nature as the dominant life form, even if it's the ethical choice. Doesn't our instinct to fight and kill inherently drive us to succeed? Isn't this a prime example of survival of the fittest? If we overcome this, it might show that we are intelligent beings capable of progress!"

"Possibly," Emmie said, "this will be shown by which species wins and where they go from there."

"May the best species win," Evelyn said quietly. The entire group sat silently, deep in thought.

CHAPTER TWENTY-FIVE

The Schizophrenic & the Heretic

DELSIN PULLED OUT HIS EARBUDS, having heard a knock on his bedroom door.

"Del!" his mother called gently as she popped her head in. "A man is at the door for you, a priest. He said he has to talk to you." Delsin looked at her, puzzled. "Should I tell him no?" she asked, knowing he'd chosen to withdraw from the public eye.

"No, Mother. Thank you." He stood up, setting his phone down. Barefoot, the plush carpet tickling his soles, he approached the door, grateful for the unfamiliar luxury he now enjoyed.

"Mr. Buck," said Father Johnson, perking up, visually taking in Delsin. The intimidating honey-skinned man stood firm in the doorway and extended his hand in a cool greeting toward the man, his face stoic. Chris took his hand, clasping it warmly with both hands, and gave it a sweaty shake, thinking, *Goodness, you could chisel ice with that jawline*. "Mr. Buck, I'm Father Christopher Johnson. It's nice to meet you. I've seen you online, and I would love to talk with you," he said, offering a gummy smile. "I've emailed you, but haven't heard back." Del stopped him right there, palm up, shaking his head, dark, silky hair hanging resolutely framing his face and shoulders.

"Father, I'm no longer doing interviews, and, to be honest, I've no interest in spiritual debates."

"Oh, no! I'm not here for that. I.... I'm sorry. I..." breaking eye contact, squinting, looking up, grasping for words. "How do I explain this?" he muttered. At this point, Christopher pinched his nose between two fingers and scrunched his nose. "Mr. Buck, may I please come in?" Hands steepled, droplets of sweat on his pink brow. Delsin sighed, having already decided to let the man in. Still, he was waiting, interested in seeing exactly how this would play out since the priest said he wasn't here to discuss his potential descent into hell or his need for exorcism. He stepped back, opening the door the rest of the way, and held out a well-built arm, offering an invitation. Chris stepped forward nervously and noticed the view of the ocean.

"Oh! That's... Oh?" Chris said, awestruck. Brown knit, his expression shifting to apprehension as he studied the sea. Delsin followed his lead, walked over to the window, put his hands in his pockets, and leaned against the frame. "It's... you can see that it's so much higher than it used to be," he said, glancing at Delsin for confirmation that what he saw was correct.

"Mm-hmm," Delsin agreed. Both men looked over the rooftops of the lower buildings, beachfront properties, and businesses, which were now submerged. Angry waves crashed violently, depositing sand onto the once-busy avenues. Meteorologists had predicted that water levels would rise rapidly as the full moon approached, and this was indeed the case. Chris brought a hand to his mouth when he saw the carrion of lifeless marine creatures—countless species of fish, crustaceans, and porpoises—washed ashore, littering the streets like trash. There were large sections of broken coral with jagged remains protruding from the sand.

Chris stammered, "I've stayed away from the water because… Well, you know. She's out there," Chris said. Delsin nodded thoughtfully. "Are you? Do you? I've watched several videos, but what I see seems different from what you see." Chris stumbled, struggling to find the right words.

"What do you see?" Delsin asked, his interest piqued. He had yet to meet anyone who might be sharing this experience with him. Delsin sat back in an armchair and motioned for Chris to sit across from him. His mother entered, bringing each man a glass of water. "Father, this is my mother, Mary.

"My son is gifted with communion with the Great Spirits. Do you speak with your god?" she asked of the priest earnestly as she perched on the sofa's edge.

"Maybe. I don't know or understand what's happening to me. At first, I thought I was sick, but it seems I'm not. Then, I thought I must be schizophrenic, but when I realized that I was seeing true events, I knew what I was experiencing was real. Although related, it doesn't seem to be the same thing you are. Delsin and his mother looked at one another, unsure what to make of this peculiar, clammy man. Chris giggled nervously as he vocalized his explanation. "I actually… become her."

"So, you are the monster? You are the one doing all of this damage?" she asked, trying to hide her amusement with the heel of her hand, setting her down her glass, interested.

"Mother!" Del said kindly. "I'm sorry," he apologized to the clergyman. "Can you explain any more?"

He stammered, then chuckled nervously, clearing his throat, and began. "I don't think that

I am a shark. I... am, a man, to be sure. However, there are times when I enter a trance, and I see through the eyes of the beast. I have been with her all along since her release." Delsin looked up at his sister at the word "release," noticing she had wandered into the common room. That was a part of the story he hadn't known, and he was judging the legitimacy of the man's story.

His sister, curious after hearing the unfamiliar voice, approached. She only knew Gideon as a guest. When her brother looked to her, she shrugged lightly, showing she didn't have an opinion yet but was open to hearing more.

Quietly, she took her place in an adjacent seat of the same room, as if to avoid imposing, signaling that she was listening but reluctant to interfere. She began to sketch, appearing uninterested, yet it was evident she was there to support her brother. Aware of the unfair treatment he'd endured since their last living together, she wanted him to know, even if she didn't fully grasp the details, that she was willing to advocate for him in any way possible. As the sun retired over the horizon, the priest shared everything he knew from beginning to end.

CHAPTER TWENTY-SIX

Confession

ADEM AND EVELYN dropped off at their loft, rushed through the blazing heat to enter the cool solace of their apartment. After grabbing a cold drink and kicking off their shoes, they quickly settled on the couch, their minds troubled but their stomachs growling for food. Neither were in the mood to cook nor for takeout.

"I have a compromise," Evelyn said, untangling herself from him on the couch.

"Where do you think you're going?" he asked, dragging her down to him for a kiss.

"We have some good cheese and crackers. I'll cut up some fruit to go along with it, and voilà, dinner will be served," she offered judiciously

"That sounds good," he agreed. "It's too hot for warm food," he said, suddenly solemn. "I've been meaning to tell you that I'm sorry for everything you went through before and during our separation." She turned toward him, observing her husband carefully. She looked at him timidly, curiously, and prodded.

"To what are you referring exactly?" she wondered if she might finally get the apology she'd been hoping for since the incident. Knowing this could get heavy really quickly, she wasn't sure she had the energy for this kind of exchange.

"The whole explosion in the lab and everything that followed. You'd told me to slow down and follow safety protocol, but I jumped ahead, and, because of my carelessness, you ended up hurt," he admitted

"Well," she reasoned, "I was there too. I could've reported you or something. So, it was as much my fault as yours."

"Reported me? Really? That's crap, and you know it," he said. "You were the one who ended up injured. If I had realized what would have happened, I never would have been so aggressive," he explained. Wrapping her arms around herself and lowering her head, she countered.

"But you knew there was potential danger. You understood you were putting both of us at risk. That's why those rules exist—to prevent anyone from getting hurt—and yet you went ahead regardless of yourself, me, or anyone else. We're fortunate no one was killed. Well, no one important anyway."

"No one important? What are you talking about?"

"No one. Nothing," she muttered, regretting the remark.

"This is news. Who died?" he questioned, standing up and approaching her. He turned to face her. He placed his finger under her chin, lifting her face so her eyes would meet his.

Don't shut me out," he begged. "This is what happened before. This is why we ended up separated."

"The reason we ended up separated had nothing to do with what I did or did not do!" she clarified coolly, shrugging his biceps off her shoulders.

"Is there someone else involved in our breakup that I don't know about?" he asked, totally caught off guard.

"There was."

"Evelyn Christine, were you...? You were seeing someone. Is that why you became so distant? Is it over, at least?" he begged. She stared at him, shooting ice daggers at him while he rubbed her arms. "Tell me, darling. I'm listening.

"I can't do this tonight. I'm going to take a bath," she said, loosening his grip from her and heading upstairs.

"I'll go with you." He followed her to the elegant bathroom with a large, claw-footed bathtub. She turned on the hot water tap, dropped in a lavender bath bomb, and lit a eucalyptus candle. She quickly pulled her long hair into a messy topknot and turned out the bright lights. She dropped her clothes into the hamper; he followed suit.

"What are you doing?" she asked incredulously.

"I'm getting in with you to give you that back rub you've been asking for."

"You hate baths!"

"BUT I love you, and I need to know what happened between us. We've already wasted too much time. I need to hear this. Whatever you have to say, I'm ready."

He stepped into the steaming water, wincing slightly at the thought of scalding his jewels, which made her crack a smile.

"Turn it down, Silly. I didn't know you were getting in." He adjusted the knobs, swished the water around, and then settled himself in. She climbed in after him and nestled between his muscular thighs. She was hesitant to relax, but couldn't help but improve her mood. She appreciated how well he understood her and knew just what to do. Joyfully, she reached for her bath oil and drizzled it all over her shoulders.

Not that stuff, he thought. Grimacing, he put his hands in the oil, disliking the feel, but reminding himself that he loved his wife. Fingers coated with oil, he began gliding his hands over her shoulders and neck, kneading the muscles. He realized he liked how his fingers moved with the emollient. His rough fingers slid over her smooth, copper skin. Getting lost in the moment, he rubbed both shoulders and began working on her neck until he heard her sigh, feeling her knots loosen and melt away.

"No matter what happened, I'm already prepared to move past it, but I need to know so it no longer stands in between us," he interjected, rousing her from a steamy daze.

"Fine. You want to know?" the woman asked, realizing that if the world was ending, she might as well state her mind. "It was obviously because of the accident that I couldn't conceive. I'm broken, barren, defective."

"Conceive? We hadn't even decided to try for a baby," he said, entirely caught off guard by this turn.

"We were talking about it. I made an appointment to get off my birth control, and the doctor had some concerns. She asked if I wanted fertility testing, so I went ahead. It was determined that the radiation I was exposed to damaged my eggs; I was devastated." He pulled her close against his chest and held her tight at this news.

"We started discussing it, and then you stopped talking about it. I thought you lost interest. You grew colder and more distant. I just thought maybe you changed your mind because you were so angry with me about whatever was bothering you. We were busy. I just thought maybe you had decided against motherhood, against having a family with me.

"No," she countered. "You brought it up three more times, making plans for our future with a child. I didn't know what to say. Me lose interest in you, the ultimate love of my life? Me, not want to bring a child into this world that's part you and part me? What wouldn't I want about that?"

"I couldn't say, and I didn't want to pressure you if that wasn't your desire. I definitely didn't want you to have a kid for me."

"I knew having a child of your own would matter to you, and then you started getting all preachy with your Bible studies. When I listened to you, it seemed like a recurring theme was how the downfall of mankind was blamed on women and how infertility was a punishment for unworthy women. It was crushing. Is that what you thought of me?

"What? No! Why would you have thought that?"

"Because you started moving away from me, and then you suddenly decided to leave the department. I thought that if you couldn't have a baby with me, you deserved a chance with someone else. So, I tried to let you go, but I thought you'd think about it and come back." She stopped talking and turned in the water so they were chest to chest. "Thoughts of you moving on with another woman tormented me."

"That's insane. The idea is crazy. Do you know that? Just because I love the idea of having a little one with you doesn't mean I would want to impregnate someone else. There was no reason for you to go through all of that alone. You should have talked to me."

"Me, crazy?" she asked, still hung up on that one word that she found the ultimate insult, tears flooding down her flushed cheeks.

"Yes, honey. Yes, but you're my crazy, and I wouldn't have it any other way. You're my beautiful, elegant, intelligent, hardworking, unique, maniac woman. You're soft and dewy but hard as nails when you need to be, and you're always evolving and becoming better than you were before. You amaze me every day! Now, let's try to make a baby," he suggested, tracing her bottom lip with his thumb and feeling his body stir at the thought.

"We can't," she lamented.

"We can't? We can't try?" he asked teasingly.

"Well, we can try, but we can't have one. Just imagine," she said.

"Who's to say for a fact? Right now, a dinosaur is planning our extinction. Who's to say what's impossible?" he asked honestly.

"I'm deformed," she said, covering her body with her hands. "I'm not even a woman anymore."

"I know things about you and would beg to differ," he said, letting his words trail off as he kissed her neck. Having this truth revealed and knowing that he still accepted and loved her unconditionally was all she needed to hear. She was his, all his. Her body went lax with cooperation.

"Okay," she whispered in his ear, arms locked around his neck, steam rising from her shoulders. He took her consent without hesitation and stood, lifting them both, water falling as if a ship was departing the sea. Laughing, she wrapped her legs around him as he boldly stepped out of the tub, arms around her, water pouring all over the tile. Giggling, she held tight like a little koala bear as he slogged across the bedroom carpet and tossed her onto the bed. Seeing her skin prickle from the cold, he decided to lie over her to warm her up, his eyes dancing. Welcoming him now that he was warm and less drippy, she laughed as he shook his head like a dog shedding water from his clean hair so it wouldn't drip onto her. This bed was where they made up for the months of lost time. They made love that night and early into the morning—madly, truly, and deeply.

CHAPTER TWENTY-SEVEN

Vanguard

ONCE THE PLAN had been devised, the team was given a seven-day break. Supplies would be collected during their absence, and travel arrangements prepared. They were instructed to go and spend time doing whatever they wished with whomever they chose, while strongly considering the possibility that their plan might fail. Michaels released them from their current contracts, issuing the following directive:

"Half of life is lost in charming others. The other half is lost in going through anxieties caused by others. Leave this play. You have played enough. -Rumi. Have fun, people. You have each been paid a sum of $ 500 million. Additionally, you will be provided with transportation to anywhere you desire and have been granted legal immunity for any petty crimes committed while on leave. I request that you not murder unnecessarily or share our government's secrets; ultimately, the choice is yours. Do what you will, and I ask that you return in 168 hours. The group was astounded by this announcement but quickly found their voices to begin stating their requests, each with a unique journey in mind.

~ Twenty Hours Later ~

The world's most prominent international leaders sat in a Global Crisis Intervention Assembly in London. Wide-eyed, they watched a collection of facts depicting the calamity, a compilation of footage illustrating worldwide decimation. Statistics flashed across the screen on a large monitor, representing the rising international death toll. Afterward, they were bombarded with a barrage of predicted implications proposed by their scientific teams from different nations.

"We've made two significant failed attempts to kill this beast, and now we've discovered that there are actually two of them," said Prime Minister of Spain Cabrera.

"We could be facing extinction if we don't work together on this one," stated US Madame President Taylor.

"I am prepared to nuke them," said Great Leader Yang of North Korea.

"And kill us all? That may not be necessary. Our research indicates that they can be isolated and killed," said French President Evans.

"We must track both animals and plan a simultaneous attack as they seem to be communicating," added Spain's Prime Minister, Cabrera.

"Kill them," agreed, President of Brazil Batista.

"We can use atomic bombs," suggested Indonesian President Kusuma. After another few hours of futile discussion, the panel voted unanimously to attempt cryogenic freezing and to detonate two neutron bombs as a failsafe once they could track them sufficiently. This needed to be orchestrated so the two would surface around the full moon as the tides flooded the beaches, utilizing beacons to lure them and radar to track them.

After the meeting, they returned to their respective countries and started working together to monitor the beasts and transport the world's last living dinosaurs to their final destination.

The American team was scheduled to report on Monday, so the plan could be put into motion. A prep team was packed up and heading abroad to a roughly salvaged marine base near the Banda Arc off the coast of Indonesia, tasked with building the towers needed to get their plan underway.

CHAPTER TWENTY-EIGHT

Alexander

ALEX WAS THE FIRST to act, wasting no time contacting his potential love interest, a woman named Xanthie, from his home office. He called her to offer a week-long visit to Paris, the City of Love; however, Alex chose to keep the roiling sore a secret to himself so he could enjoy a carefree weekend with his impromptu date. She happily accepted his offer. *Better late than never,"* was her response, asking what took him so long. Within hours, they were whisked overseas on a private jet.

Once they landed, unpacked, and rested for a few hours, they headed to The Butte Montmartre, home of artists, musicians, dancers, and old films. They admired the architecture of the Sacré-Coeur while enjoying the views.

"Montmartre's charm lies in its history," he drawled as they walked lazily side by side like familiar lovers. Smiling, they observed the city of the Belle Époque, its interesting people, charming little cafes, and quaint shops. They wandered in and out of tiny brasseries tasting desserts, sipping espresso, and getting lost in the atmosphere.

On the second day, they traced the loving engravings on The Wall of Love, tucked away in Jehan Rictus Square, where hundreds of declarations of love were written in many languages. Feeling reflective, they explored the peaceful garden of the Museum of Romantic Life. They crossed the Pont des Arts, the Love Lock Bridge, and left their own padlock as a physical symbol of their current feelings. They talked about their first impressions of each other, and she delved deeper into why he had waited so long to make his move.

They were allowed into the Palace Dauphine with little government interference. They lingered in the Square du Vert Galant, where they enjoyed crystalline waters, and he stole a kiss or two, surrounded by the elegant greenery of the gardens. That night, they sipped coffee under the shelter of the hotel's awning from their balcony, cuddled under a blanket, watching barges peacefully float past as gulls called in the distance. Alex noted the rising water levels, but everything remained peaceful.

Their favorite place to visit during the week was Parc Montsouris. They found a quiet bench near the water, where they relaxed in the shade. Unzipping his pack, he tossed a blanket onto the lush grass and sat down, crossing his legs and patting the ground. He invited her to join him. Delighted by this sweet surprise, she kicked off her shoes. She closed her eyes, toes sinking into the cool, lush grass, taking note of the sensation. Flipping back through her memory book of perceptions, she couldn't remember feeling this way since she was a kid. Taking her time, she consciously enjoyed the feeling on her toes in the dappled shade. He leaned back, encouraging her to do the same. She placed one forearm over her eyes for shade, relaxing completely with her companion.

“Have you decided that I am not going to murder you yet?” he asked her in good humor, considering they were relatively new acquaintances.

“I have,” she replied without hesitation.

“So, you agreed to travel abroad with me before you knew? A woman can never be too careful these days," he chided.

“Yes, you passed my test the third time I met you almost a year ago.”

“You've been testing me?”

“I have!” she confessed. “I mean, how could

I agree to a proposal of marriage from someone who may be a serial killer?" she asked him. At this, he bolted upright.

"Marriage? When did this enter the equation?" He was intrigued.

"This isn't just fantasy. I'm a statistician. It's a prediction based on your behavior. You've wanted to ask me out since the Geneva meeting, but chickened out after seeing me accept a date from someone else. You took too long, so I decided to push you by presenting a rival, but you backed off. Then you were finally going to ask me out on your last trip last month, but then you got whisked away on some secret mission," she explained.

"Damn. You've got it all figured out," he mused.

Well, I don't know where you've been or what you've been up to, but it's serious because you haven't relaxed this entire time, regardless of how charming I am or how comfortable we've been with each other. Plus, I'm hot as hell. I mean, all your dreams have come true here, and yet you're worrying about… whatever.

"Yeah. I have been a little tense. Sorry about that," he said, rolling over. He propped himself up on one elbow to face her.

"So, when's this wedding going to take place?" he asked, utterly confused.

"Well, we're not super young, but I still need to put you through the paces to make sure you can keep up with me, so we were going to date for nine months and then be engaged for a year, but that was twelve months ago. So, you're running behind schedule. The way I see it now, you have six months to court me and then pop the question. It doesn't have to all be trips abroad, but I'll need some excitement because we'll settle down and have two kids before I'm thirty-two, and I'm nearly thirty." At this, he raised his eyebrows, sucked a deep breath in, and lay back, closing his eyes.

"Okay!" Apparently, I didn't surprise you.

"Yes, and we're going to have a long, mostly happy marriage, and you're probably going to have a heart attack and die despite staying fit and healthy when you're around sixty-three." At this, his eyes widened. "Yes, I hacked into your family's medical history, but I'll still live into my nineties. So, I plan to date as a widow and likely remarry, which our daughters will support because I was a dutiful wife. They will be strong, independent women who understand that I deserve happiness."

"Really?" he sat up, studying her expression.

She pulled her arm away from her face, locking eyes with him, and then erupted with laughter at the look on his face. "Are you going to kiss me or what?" she finally asked point-blank. Swooping in, he cut her off by grazing his lips over hers. Reaching her arms around his neck and pulling him down to her breast, with some coaxing, she allowed him to kiss her deeply. When the couple came up for air, she was giggling.

"Finally, you relaxed!" she remarked.

"Well, why should I worry about anything when you've got it all figured out?" he asked.

"You don't," she responded confidently.

"Okay, then," he acquiesced, genuinely gladdened by the idea but also sad. He lay back down next to her.

"So, tell me about our kids," he urged, one silent tear rolling down his cheek, which she missed. Her eyes skyward, she watched the clouds as she described the children who would never come to fruition. As she chattered on, telling him what their daughters were likely to look like and behave like, he reflected that this woman, and all women and all men, for that matter, would not be very long for this world.

"Well, we'll have two girls, eighteen months apart, Maia and Morgan, and they'll be beautiful and smart. I mean, look at us. They will have hit the jackpot. They will be the apple of your dad's eye and like second kids to my parents. My parents are younger than your dad, she pointed out. I know your mother has already passed away. I am sorry for that," she whispered, squeezing his hand.

She went on animatedly for several minutes, lost in the manifestation of her future projections for her future with this man, whom she had yet to claim as her own technically. As the sun softened, the two fell asleep in each other's arms, shadows traveling across their bodies as the afternoon expired, one day closer to potential doom.

The following day, they stayed in bed and ordered room service, touring each other's childhoods and discovering surprising things about each other. He used to sing in a heavy metal band. That made her laugh heartily, teasing him about all of the women with whom he likely dallied.

Rested, they dressed, ate a sumptuous lunch downstairs, and then visited a traditional English garden with primeval trees, ponds, and waterfalls. Here is where he learned about her education abroad, as well as more of her hopes for the future that she was certain was ahead of them. As knowledgeable as she was, she was not privy to the fate that lay ahead.

They explored various gardens and museums on horse-drawn carriages. They relaxed while dining on the banks of the Seine River and admired the architecture of Le Meurice. They enjoyed a walking tour of Montmartre, whispering secrets as they shared rich crème caramel. As the moon rose and the world turned, he decided to live in the moment. For now, they were safe inside their hotel, tucked away comfortably. They bathed, warmed each other, and gently tumbled between cool flaxen linen.

CHAPTER TWENTY-NINE

Nomads

EMMIE ASKED TJ if he would spend his week with her. He responded that wild horses couldn't drag him away. She leaped when he suggested they go to Greece. They had gotten to know each other well and discovered they shared a love for travel. After being spirited away, the couple checked into their room and excitedly explored the hotel, discussing the esoteric architectural features they noticed throughout the halls. Their hotel looked like a historic building, with every hallway and piece of furniture belonging in a museum. It made them feel as if they were living in another time, one less dangerous. They wasted no time tossing their bags into the room and heading out into the moonlit night. They walked the streets side-by-side, pointing and talking as they admired the charming details of the city.

Smells of spices, fresh fruits, and coffee from the warmly lit buildings and taverns piqued their appetite. Suddenly realizing they were famished, they wandered into a café and ordered whatever the waitress recommended, not even asking what it was. Tension eased as they grazed on a basket of Spanakopita. Emmie picked up a triangle of warm, buttery, flaky phyllo filled with feta, dill, and cooked spinach.

Her cheeks puckered at the zest of lemon. TJ leaned forward, opening his beak like a baby bird. She stuffed an enormous piece in his mouth, giggling. He closed his eyes, laughing, relishing the taste. They thoroughly enjoyed the exotic aromas of their meal as they sipped richly aromatic drinks and talked intimately as the evening deepened into night. They were pleasantly surprised by the savory piquancy as they explored their meals and nibbled off each other's plates comfortably.

They studied the other intently. Emmie caught herself smiling at his bushy, expressive eyebrows. He animatedly told stories about his childhood, describing his antics in school, sharing memories of life with his parents and siblings, growing up in an underdeveloped country in humble conditions, and all about his ragtag group of friends. Emmie winced as he recounted details about his brother, who had recently passed away. That explained why Jasir's absence still didn't feel real. He seemed to be in shock over it, and she decided to let him be for now. Surprisingly, she learned he had briefly worked as a pilot in Saudi Arabia.

In turn, he enjoyed watching her long, delicate fingers as she recounted her childhood stories. She described how her father taught her woodworking—building a deck one winter and crafting custom furniture in the summer. TJ looked at her face, trying to tell if she was joking when she mentioned watching her strong-as-an-ox father drill through his finger with a power tool, but not stopping his work on the staircase. The man only asked her for a headlamp since the sun had set, and he obviously couldn't see anymore. Emmie added that her grandfather, a carpenter, had cut off his pointer finger years ago and had treated it just as casually.

"Off?" was the only question he asked.

"Off," she clarified. "He picked it up, wrapped his bloody stump in a dusty shop towel, and put the digit in his pocket so he could keep working." So, a drill through the finger was considered a minimal affair among the men in her family. TJ was genuinely unsure what to make of that story. His initial thought was *barbarians*. Admirable legends of her heroic father soon morphed into tender memories of being curled up next to her mother, lovingly reading children's stories about a boy and his Pooh bear, a good dog named Carl, and fantastical fairy tales from generations past. She repeated funny stories of beloved pets and sacred places in which she once played. He was captivated by the shapely curve of her lips, her finely knit brows, and the shimmer in her glossy eyes as she became somewhat emotional recalling these moments. The memories were bittersweet, with the realization that her entire family's extinction was imminent if they failed. They ended the night soaking in the private hot tub outside their room, the crisp night air caressing and teasing their bare skin.

The following morning, the two hailed a taxi at dawn and began their adventure. They hiked to the great St. Stephen Monastery in Meteora, which seemed artfully frozen in time. This was the only monastery visible from Kalambaka and had been a place of pilgrimage for nearly 10,000 years. This sacred site has a long history of miracles, and it was here that the two knelt in meditative prayer. They prayed for success once their plan was in motion. They begged for the preservation of their species. They pleaded for their families' well-being and asked for wisdom and peace of mind if these days or weeks were to be their final moments. The monks meditating there spoke of the two in Hellēnikḗ, noting their youth, positive energy, and divine fate to have fallen in love during such a dire time. A third man joined them as the trio walked away, debating in their native language whether it was a good time for mankind to die off in their native language.

"It's been too long, and man has done a poor job. It is time for our planet to experience cleansing and rebirth," the tallest one argued. After a circular debate, they all essentially agreed with him. This structure had seen thousands of men come before these two. This ancient monastery no longer shone as it had in its former glory. It had been defaced through multiple wars. In its golden years, it served as a nunnery and later became a museum, displaying ancient relics and artifacts from another era.

Two days later, they stood breathlessly in the ancient Temple of Poseidon, holding each other as she shed tears of awe, the warm breeze from the ocean teasing their senses. He watched her with smoldering fascination. As they explored, she ran her hands over ancient relics. In Skala Erresos, they played sweet games in the town square with the locals, just like children. They stuffed their bellies full of foreign delicacies in the charming village of Chalki, a place worlds away from anything else. Fortunately, in these remote areas, the crisis hadn't yet affected them, and these little villages seemed unaware of the ticking time bomb about to explode. The next night, amid the magic of the Naxos countryside, they finally consummated their budding relationship. From then on, they stayed within the walls of their hotel, content to explore the heart rather than the world.

CHAPTER THIRTY

Dru

DRU took a direct flight from DC to her family home in North Carolina. At the airport, she ran straight into the arms of her anxious boyfriend. She broke into a run as soon as she spotted him in the terminal. He instinctively wrapped his arms around her protectively, crooning.

"Carwyn," she cried.

"Sweetheart?" he embraced her strongly with

brawny arms, happy to see her but perplexed at her upset. She was often a frustratingly pragmatic young woman. He'd never seen her less than level-headed in public in all their years. She usually chose the path of logic in the face of heated disagreement. When she was selected to work on this team, the initial part of the assignment was a confidentiality agreement, accompanied by stacks of contracts, each enclosed with red tape and surmounted by threats of imprisonment in the case of a potential breach. For this reason, he was oblivious to the top-secret project she'd been working on.

Now that she was home, circumstances had shifted. Upon her return, Dru called her immediate family together, along with Carwyn, and shared the dire news. She began by plainly stating that she had life-threatening information to share. Taking her time, she first told them about each team member she'd been working with. Laughing, she described each one with their unique traits and quirks, Anton being the most eccentric and peculiar. TJ, the young foreign geologist. Alex, the handsome but somber businessman. Emmie is an elegant and diligent biology researcher. The married scientists were romantic goals in her view; they made a perfectly complementary pair and were so intelligent. After describing the intense secrecy she had to maintain and how she met each of her colleagues, she digressed by detailing every preemptive thought that had ever crossed her mind. Tucked safely in her parents' lodge, they all sat on edge, overwhelmed by worry about what threat was menacing their only child.

Finally, nervously gathering her curly locks behind her ears with one hand on Carwyn's shoulder for support, she recounted the lengthy story of what the cadre had learned. She wept as she described the brutal genocide she had witnessed and summarized the predictions of future events. Everyone sat in silence, their gazes fixed. They looked at each other for clues on how to react; Carwyn pulled Dru close and held her tightly as she sobbed uncontrollably, exhausting herself.

From his slouched position on the couch, her little brother began texting, appearing unfazed. Her father stood and started pacing, asking silly questions, while her mother spun her ring around her finger. Feeling weak, her mother lowered her head into her hands and quietly rocked, wiping tears from her rosy cheeks. The next hour was spent answering unanswerable questions in a rapid-fire manner. Finally, her little brother, bored with the logistics, interrupted and shifted the entire mood.

"D, you're saying the world is ending, like, soon?"

"Yes," She answered, squared-shouldered, not bothering to mince words.

"So... YOLO. I mean, let's do whatever we want," he suggested, simply looking around the room at the dramatic upheaval. Family members examining each other, and they agreed. Her father shrugged and started preparing an authentic Indian dinner. Her mother blew her nose, loosening her shoulders in resignation. Dru was shocked at the idea. She was fully committed to a sorrowful reunion with her loved ones and a bleak, last few days. She had already decided not to shoulder the burden alone, regardless of the circumstances.

"Dru," Carwyn interrupted, holding her hand and getting down on one knee, "Will you do me the honor of..."

"Yes!" She shrieked, jumping off the couch and toppling him backward. "Let's get married!"

Her mother turned, her mouth hanging open in response to this unexpected turn of events.

"We are going to begin planning a wedding this week?" her father inquired, smiling, as the ingredients in his cookware began to steam, filling the room with tantalizing fragrances.

"Tomorrow." She announced matter-of-factly. "We are getting married tomorrow." Dialing Michaels, she made a few calls. The Pentagon will have it all arranged.

When alone with her fiancé, she apologized for the times she was difficult or put her journey before his. She shared her true feelings, explaining that she didn't always feel brave and calm, but she believed she had something to prove and felt she had to act that way. Then, she asked to be comforted and caressed while there was still time. Early the next day, a phone call was scheduled for a wedding by the president's order at six that evening. Without worries, she took a long, luxurious bath, thinking about how beautiful her wedding gown would be. A wedding, a honeymoon, all in the next few days—though they would be brief. Although filled with happiness, the events were overshadowed by the grief of what may soon come.

Come evening, she found herself walking arm in arm with her father down a gravel path between rustic chairs filled with the faces of everyone she'd ever known and loved at Hawkesdene Estate in Andrews, North Carolina. The lush, aromatic bouquets of lilies and roses scented the grounds. She was wrapped in a magnificent ivory gown featuring a sheer lace bodice and a plunging off-the-shoulder neckline. It shimmered from every angle with sequins, pearls, and beads, highlighting her slim yet healthy silhouette. Everyone watched reverently as she floated down the aisle, showcasing the couture low-backed gown with silk-covered buttons and a Vpattern that echoed the chapel-length train.

The father kissed the bride and gave her away, the toe-headed ring bearer produced the ring, the candles were lit, and the sweethearts made their claims and proclamations of all they would do for their entire lives, whether that be one week or one century. The trees high above them created a shady canopy, leaves trembled, whispering well wishes to the young couple as they said, 'I do.' They kissed deeply as they were pronounced man and wife, and the pastor presented the exquisite couple. The spellbound audience stood, erupting with applause, moved by the magic that hung in the air.

Through glimmering eyes, Dru gazed into the audience, tears threatening to ruin her flawless makeup. She took a deep breath and smiled at the crowd of spectators, choosing her favorites: Grandma Dot, Aunt Sue, Bea, Rover, all the cousins she grew up with, and her closest college friends. Even her brother was clapping and smirking in approval of this milestone. When she looked closer, she realized he was staring amorously at the ample cleavage of her maid of honor, which made her laugh at the poor kid.

That night, the newlyweds tried to soak in every memory of the festivities as the moments passed by. A band played while the guests dined and danced on the terrace. They chuckled as the flower girl scampered across the dance floor, chasing the ring bearer with a sparkler. He shrieked with laughter, golden ringlets flying as he galloped past, tapping in his black patent dress shoes, knocking over the purse of an older woman who was nibbling cake at her table.

As the sun set, torches were lit, and fairy lights twinkled. It was enchanting. The warm air and beautiful venue were enough to make a bride feel as if this night marked the start of wonderful things to come. She tried hard not to think about what might happen next. After a few hours, the moon rose, and the bride and groom slipped away to walk the path down to the dock.

"Are you okay walking these planks in those crazy shoes?" he asked tenderly, concerned for his new wife, not wanting to break her the first moment he'd relinquished her from her parents. She pulled her skirts up, chuckling as she wriggled her toes at the end of a bare foot. "When did that happen?" he asked dubiously. "I thought the shoes were like the crowning jewel of the dress," he reasoned.

"They were," she smiled, hopping down the steps toward the lakeside double-footed and fancy-free. "Which is why I was wearing them through the whole wedding and took them off the second the last ceremony photo was taken. Twirling.

"You didn't even notice that I was six inches shorter when we were dancing," she pointed out.

"Well, you were regular size. So, I guess I completely forgot about the shoes," he realized.

"And so did everyone!" she craftily pointed out, grinning. "My love?" she queried, her voice turning husky.

"Yes, Kitten?" he replied, reaching for her in the dark, suddenly feeling serious.

Did you marry me just because the world is ending?

"Not even a little bit," he stated dutifully. "I wanted cake," he explained.

"What?" she snorted.

"Not just any cake, though. Like, a bakery-quality gourmet cake made for a once-in-a-lifetime event with baby blue icing. Pastels taste better than any other colors. I'm not sure why." He paused mid-diatribe to see why she wasn't protesting. He looked down at her with her hands on her hips, eyes glimmering, trembling lips. "I'm kidding!" he assured, grappling her in a rough cuddling hug, and she began to bawl.

"I know you are," she sobbed. "You're just so damn silly," she resolved. "No matter what, you always know how to counter my seriousness and lighten the mood. You are my helpmate, ally, best friend, teammate, confidant, match, and soulmate. Carwyn Connor Kelly, you are my everything, and I am so honored to have become your wife," she said, sniffling.

"Well, yeah," he replied, reassuring her in his smooth way.

"Can we go to bed now?" she begged, "I'm suddenly very, very tired." He pulled her close, kissed her warm, damp forehead, nodding. With that, husband and wife left the reception together without saying goodnight and went to their rapturous honeymoon suite, from which they did not emerge until late afternoon the next day. It was a good choice if this night had to be one of their last.

CHAPTER THIRTY-ONE

The Docs

Adem and Evelyn quickly took off, heading back to their cozy home off the California coast. When they arrived, they were greeted by the strong, welcoming scent of the forest and the sea; they also saw a very excited Kanik barking enthusiastically at the gate, on a leash held by an annoyed driver.

The couple retrieved him from his chaperone, nearly knocked backward by big dog hugs. Adem picked him up and skillfully hoisted the massive malamute over his right shoulder as he went up the stairs two at a time. This display of balance and strength earned him admiration. The dog-sitter shook his head, shocked, as he got into his car, leaving with a $1,000,000 tip.

When the father and son entered the house, the man skillfully flipped the dog onto its back, cradling him like a giant baby, asking if he was a stinky boy while Daddy was away. Kanik howled, chuffed, and groaned, recounting every painful detail of his owners' absence. Evelyn watched the dramatic scene unfold, tears in her eyes at the reunion as she ruffled the dog's belly fluff. She buried her face in his mane and opened her arms to enfold both of them. She mewled softly, realizing the time she had wasted during the months of separation. Over what? Petty grudges. At that moment, she only wished to let go of the regret and fill her heart with the joy of their reunion.

"What's this?" Adem inquired, smiling as he squeezed the massive dog between him and his mate so he could balance the dog while reaching one arm around his quietly sobbing wife.

"I just… I'm so sorry," she said between racking breaths.

"Sorry? For missing our dog, our only child?" he joked good-naturedly.

"The child? It really wasn't your fault that we never conceived. I don't know if that had anything to do with my infertility. I've blamed you all this time, but the truth is, there was plenty of time long before that. It's a wonder I didn't get pregnant in college.

"Now? That's what you're worried about now? Given the state of the world, perhaps it's a blessing we never had a baby. How could we focus on the problem at hand if we were worried about the welfare of our child or children?" he asked pragmatically.

"I guess... maybe," she agreed logically. "But all this time, I told myself that you were to blame, and I worried that you would feel unfulfilled, tethered to some wasteland of a woman. I worried that you wouldn't be satisfied with just me for your whole life. How could you want to grow old with a defective partner?"

"Defective?" he asked, pulling away from

her, letting Kanik slide to the floor, and taking her face in both hands as he often did. "Who's to say that our lack of children isn't my fault, and what would make you think I would ever need more than we already have?" he asked sensibly. Cocking one eyebrow seriously, "and if all of this insanity has been running through your mind the last year, why haven't we been talking about it?" She lowered her eyes, considering the ramifications of her behavior.

"Hmmm?" he probed lovingly.

"Forgive me?" she murmured into his shoulder.

"Only, if you can forgive me for not realizing what you've been going through. And… for my arrogance," he added. She trembled, left shaken by his love, understanding, and pure devotion.

"How?" she asked, gazing into his eyes.

"How, what?" he inquired, a smile quirking his lips.

"How…" She let go of him and spun around their kitchen with arms raised overhead, "--did I become so lucky?" Merrily, hair flying, she whirled back into his arms. "You truly are my soulmate, and if the world is going to end, I'm glad to be with you, and I want to make the best of our last days together." Kanik frolicked on his hind legs, still celebrating their reunion.

"Let's not talk about what may come. Let's just… spend time together," he suggested.

"Yes. Let's," she agreed, happily embracing a peace she had not experienced in too long. As evening sprawled gently around them, they ordered dinner from their favorite

Brazilian grill. It was delivered in record time by two unnamed FBI agents. Relishing, they opened the containers. The savory steam wafting enticed them to dig in with abandon. While they stuffed themselves, Adem looked after his wife lovingly.

They ate. She drank spirits. They danced to their old records wrapped only in knitted blankets, with Kanik joining in and howling his own version of each song. The cheerful trio ended the evening breathing in the cool, crisp air while stargazing from the upper deck. They lingered outside, darkness softly surrounding them until the chill forced them inside and upstairs to their bedroom. They collapsed into bed together with Kanik pressed closely beside them. He felt the need to touch both of them after their long separation. Soon enough, the silly dog was snoring and whimpering in his sleep, his paws softly thumping as he dreamed of quick furry things darting just out of reach.

Hours later, the sun gently woke them from their intertwined sleep. The lovers stirred, stretched, bathed, and went downstairs for a simple breakfast. Kanik stepped out for his morning duel with red squirrels. As morning brightened, they flirted, teased, and taunted each other just like they had in years past, nibbling on toast and sipping hot drinks. Breakfast ended with tender love play on the kitchen island, after which they both felt hungry but emotionally fulfilled. After a proper breakfast together, they took a winding walk from their cabin into the forest with no set plan. They huffed hand-in-hand hiking uphill, their breath puffing out like clouds, while the trail was wide, and Kanik happily marked the path along the way. As the trail curved around the hill and narrowed, Adem instinctively took the lead. The three of them headed upward. He waited patiently while his beloved paused to sketch the various shapes of leaves and trees, trying to capture all the shades of green and textures of the wood. Amused, he noticed her stopping just as lactic acid began to burn in his muscles from the strenuous uphill climb. His mouth twitched as he watched her gather pine cones along the way, only selecting those she found noteworthy. To him, they looked the same, but she happily stashed them in her pack, grinning at her collection.

When her pack was heavy to bursting, he turned her around, took the bag from her behind her, and shouldered it upon himself, tenderly saying, "That's enough." She was elated.

The forest floor grew pleasantly warm as the sun rose and burned off the morning fog. Having reached a small summit, he was filled with affection as he watched her tilt her head back, squinting and looking, trying to identify which birds were calling. The woman perched atop a large rock and unzipped her jacket. Just as they became damp with sweat, they reached the water's edge of the large pond. With no discussion except a cheeky look of agreement, the couple stripped out of their clothes, abandoning them on tree branches, and skinny-dipped in the crisp, calm lake. They splashed, wrestled, and squealed playfully in the clear water. Half-heartedly, the wolf-dog lingered at the water's edge, fishing for minnows and blowing bubbles with his snout. He soon found a pebbled spot to sit and watch his owners, one ear cocked in the sphinx pose, diligently scouring the pads of his feet. He skillfully removed small burs from the thick fur between his toes with bared teeth. When the couple tired, they sunbathed bare-skinned on a wide, sun-kissed boulder, eventually dozing next to each other. Awakened when the sun was high, they were dry and snickered as they peeled their saliferous skin from the toasty rocks, noting the damp impressions left behind by their bodies. They stepped back, critiquing each other's wet impressions. She complimented him on the wingspan of his shoulders, a trait she'd always admired. He praised her for her ample, heart-shaped imprint and the delicate footprints that traveled from her resting spot back into the water. Clad somewhat haphazardly, they easily made their way back down the hill.

When they reached home again, they were starving. Fish and vegetables were delivered fresh from the market with one quick call. Adem grilled as Evelyn painted on an easel out on the terrace, wearing nothing more than his worn T-shirt. Once, she gripped the collar and drank in the scent of him, his essence thick on the t-shirt he'd dampened with his pheromone-drenched perspiration. As the sun set, he guessed at the species of native plants that had begun to take shape on her canvas, inspired by the aerial view of the forest from their porch. They ate their fill and wandered up to bed early in the spirit of enjoying a quiet evening together.

As she undressed, he opened every bedroom window at her request. Snuggled together, covered in plush down, they relaxed. In their sleeping positions: her cheek against his strong chest, delicate shoulder tucked warmly under his broad wing, their legs intertwined, she drifted into sleep. As the night deepened, they were soothed by the rustling leaves and the sounds of the night. She gently dozed like a tiny bird. He stayed awake, stroking her hair as he listened to her slow, steady breathing. He reflected on his accomplishments, goals, and dreams—those he had achieved and others that had been forgotten over his lifetime. An unexpected tear rolled down his cheek, and he felt that he had lived his life well. His parents were proud. He had positively influenced his students and was loved by an extraordinary, energetic scholar whose passion burned as brightly as his own. Although he had no children to carry on his bloodline, his species would likely become extinct soon. Not having a child to worry about was actually a blessing. As sleep overtook him, he decided he had no regrets and, if it were possible to do it all again, he would repeat it all, perhaps with a little more patience. He and this woman had built a beautiful life.

They slept late the next day and spent an idle morning indoors, only half-dressed, reminiscing about their favorite memories passed. They borrowed an Appaloosa quarter horse and a palomino Friesian from the neighbor in the afternoon. They rode horseback on the coast until dusk, when they sat around a fire, poking the coals of the beach bonfire until they were sleepy.

On their last full day in their sanctuary, they copied photographs, collected memorabilia, wrote snippets of their memoirs, recorded their final wishes in journals, and placed them in a time capsule. The four federal agents assigned to dig the hole were less than thrilled by the task, which only made the project more entertaining.

Their last night, they stayed awake all night, erotically tormenting each other in every room of the house, laughing, moaning, and trembling, reaching peaks they'd yet to achieve before. They worshipped each other in unison as if this night were their last. During these final days at home, they said goodbye with their bodies but never with words, deliberately avoiding any actions that might shift the balance of fate against them.

The morning they were scheduled to report, they gathered for a slow breakfast of fruits and pastries on the balcony, which they found on the porch after Kanik woke them barking. They stayed there barely dressed until their escorts arrived, insisting they were behind schedule and that their chopper was waiting. When the lead agent finally threw a rock with a note on top of the balcony, announcing they were preparing to contact Michaels, they wandered inside to get dressed and grab their bags.

CHAPTER THIRTY-TWO

Banda Arc

ON A WINDY MONDAY MORNING, the plan was set in motion. The team had returned and flown abroad to a roughly salvaged marine base on the Banda Arc off the coast of Indonesia. Upon touchdown, they were dropped off hastily onto the helipad. The sea spattered them as the wind tore angrily at them. They could see military teams assembling guns and catapults with sedatives and caging. They were hurried off the aircraft, water licking at their heels.

"The pilots said they could only land here unless the pad were still above water, and, as you can see, the water is rising," Michaels yelled over the turbines. Evelyn and Adem looked at each other, their dismay clear. "How we escape from here, I hope, will be a problem for another day," he replied after noticing their expressions. This idea made Evie's chest tighten with anxiety, worsened by the rocky helicopter ride. Intentionally, she pushed the concern out of her mind, knowing they might or might not have a tomorrow. They escaped the noise of the aircraft as it lifted from its perch and followed the chaos of trucks and generators to the job site. The group found the two lead officials already engaged in discussion. They were directed toward their tent and told to put down their bags and put on their boots.

Dru entered their fort with a handful of Styrofoam cups and some hot cocoa mix as dusk settled. This was the best I could do. The crew was troubleshooting at two card tables, with the wind whipping around their tent, seeming to mimic their distress.

A strange mix of optimism and dread besieged the friends, heavily laden with their plans. They'd been back aground for only a few hours before sat studies began to show increased activity in the region, ensuring this was an ideal location to set their trap. Having been away for the past week, they felt somewhat recharged and ready to face the giantess after their break.

As they brainstormed, they listened through headsets to sound bites from Anton expressing increased concern over skyrocketing temperatures, rising water levels, and the growing acidity of the water. Hellish freak storms were swirling around, causing unprecedented disasters on every continent. There were reports from Mexico where citizens were being battered to death by basketball-sized hail. Tornadoes, hurricanes, and earthquakes plagued the United States; floods and mudslides affected Germany. Volcanoes were erupting in Russia and Iceland. South China lost thousands after being caught off guard by freezing cyclones. Snow fell in the jungles of Brazil, and the Arctic was sinking under warming waters. The oceans advanced over the coasts, and vengeful winds shrieked across the landscape, uprooting farmland. Mother Nature was leaving a malevolent trail of destruction behind.

"What about the trance that sharks are supposed to enter when turned upside down?" Emmie asked. "Is that a myth?"

"No. That's been proven, but this species is unique from other currently living animals in so many ways that we can't count on anything that we think we know," Adem replied.

"So, the infinydon has been dormant for the last what billion years?" TJ asked.

"Mmm… let's say 2.5 to 3.6 million or so." Evelyn conjectured, raising her voice over the ever-increasing wind. "The planet went through a period of climate change in which the environment cooled down. Many species failed to survive into the next era."

"There are two areas of suspected weakness we plan to focus on," Adem said. "In over 10 million years of roaming our Earth, this species has left fossilized teeth on the coasts of every continent except Antarctica. It would seem unlikely she can survive the cold."

"Secondly, a shark's liver keeps them buoyant. Once removed or injured to the point of dysfunction, they can no longer swim up and down, debilitating them," Evelyn relayed.

"If we can capture her, we're hoping to be able to exploit one of these areas?" Adem stated.

"That's the plan," Dru asked.

"What is the plan exactly?" Alex asked.

"The plan is to bait her, capture her, and injure her liver," Evelyn determined.

"Yes, but given her ferocity to this point, we'd be fools to think that this alone will work. So, the next step is to debilitate her with liquid nitrogen and freeze her to death." TJ explained.

"We have 100 pressurized, super-insulated vacuum vessels of the fluid ready for injection once she's been shot. We're going to suspend her animation completely," Emmie reported.

"And how are we going to bait her?" asked Adem, taking a long drink from his water bottle.

Present-day sharks can detect vibrations in the water using a special organ called the lateral line. They also possess an incredible sense of smell, which enables them to communicate through molecules moving across the mucous membrane of the nose. "We'll use vibrations to lure her into the area and then the chum to bring her into the trap," Evelyn explained.

~ Eighteen Hours Later ~

Weapons were built, and the aquatic resonance speaker transmitted vibratory signals to signal the beast. Adem and Evelyn were on watch in an observation tower. Emmie and TJ were resting in the bunkhouse. Alex and Dru were gathering items for a meal in the makeshift mess hall when Adem noticed the seismograph start to shake.

"Honey, take a peek at the sat footage. Do you see anything?" After reading the measures, she activated the com system.

"Delta Zulu, Cthulhu Incoming!" she announced on the radio. As the research team assembled and shared the readings, the military troops, led by Michaels, were gathering as two uniformed individuals entered the tower. With

Alex right behind, Dru was the first to rush into the building. Emmie and TJ tumbled in just after, rubbing sleep from their eyes.

"Dr. Humboldt," the formidable gentleman implored. The husband and wife both turned around. The man was built like a tank and dressed in a sharp uniform, dripping with sashes and pendants, which proclaimed him a supreme hero.

"Dr. Evelyn Humboldt," he said. "I'm told you're the lead researcher on this assignment." Looking at her husband for feedback, Adem gave none. He shrugged, palms up, shaking his head. She, too, responded with a shrug.

"Am I?" she asked. The team had not been briefed or interacted with except when necessary. Politics or procedures were heavily glossed over as their focus was paramount.

"Yes. I'm Commander in Chief Jean Pierre Sibblies, overseeing this operation." A striking woman half his size, looking twice as harsh, in an orderly navy coat and trousers with a single-breasted jacket. The single row of four gold-colored buttons gleamed, decorated with rows of gold sleeve stripes, badges, and service stripes, indicating that she was a force to be reckoned with. The curly-haired, compact commander extended her hand.

I'm Secretary of the Navy, Elizabeth Torres. I'm overseeing the marine snare. I'm primarily here to assist with damage control. Based on the information available, our chances of success are below 10%. What is your assessment?

"I would say that's accurate," Evelyn

admitted. The tension in the air thickened visibly at that report. "And it seems as if we have an incoming heading our way. The troops are readying the trap, and we should have eyes on the target in a few minutes." She pointed to the satellite projections showing a large target beeping and traveling ever closer. Sibblies pursed his lips before clenching and releasing his fists at his sides, while Torres stretched to stand a bit taller, preparing for what was to come.

The fear of the great unknown was intense. At this moment, Adem unlocked some orange bins with life jackets and began handing them out. The scientists and military personnel fastened each buckle and adjusted it to ensure a proper fit. Next, Adem strapped a floating pack to his wife and then tethered them together with an elastic cord.

“Wherever you go, I go too,” he whispered to her.

“I love you,” she answered without taking her eyes off the scene.

Navy pilots from thirty different aerial locations were armed with cannon-like harpoon guns as the mass approached. It was then that they saw a vast fin breach the water half a mile away. Evelyn was at the computer, snapping infrared images that showed the infinydon’s body seemed to have grown since the last footage they saw of her.

“Michaels, she’s grown!” she called over the radio. "We’re going to need all of the canisters of nitrogen.” Michaels didn’t wait to break the connection or ask any follow-up questions before he started barking orders for the rest of the canisters to be distributed. The inaudible echo vibrating into the sea resonated clearly, beckoning the leviathan. Within minutes, the beast covered the distance and swam into the bay, into surprisingly shallow water. 50-gallon drums of chum were released to distract her and keep her occupied. As the water began to turn cherry, she flailed wildly. She couldn't swim well and started pushing back into deeper water growing frantic.

"Teams Alpha, Bravo, Charlie: Fire!" Michaels commanded. In almost perfect unison, the harpoon guns were discharged, there was the briefest moment of whirring on cable, and then, despite fierce thudding sounds, most of the metal spears fell away from her, unable to penetrate her armored flesh. A few had embedded superficially. Those that had reached an impact point along the border of the scale loculation were behind the pectoral fin. Noting this, Adem picked up his radio.

"They have to aim for the vulnerable areas between the scales." Knowing that heavy-duty weapons didn't have that type of precision aim on a thrashing, moving target, the leader gave the following orders.

"Teams Delta, Echo, Foxtrot: Fire!" Michaels shouted. She started to twist her body wildly, swaying side to side like a salmon slipping from a grizzly's grasp. Waves crashed against the towers' supports, and she knocked out one of the lookout peaks with her tail, which held four gunmen. They were thrown into the air and fell to their deaths. Propelled from the south tower, one of the cables pierced behind her dorsal fin. With a quick twist, the cable snapped and whipped back like an electric lasso, cutting down everything in its path.

As Dru looked down from the observation deck, close enough to feel the saltwater spray mist her face, her mouth dropped open as she stared at a uniformed figure without a torso, momentarily exterminated like a roach before collapsing into a heap in front of her. Many other bodies were scattered around. People began yelling but refused to leave their posts.

Adem noticed the commotion she was causing was splashing the water up and out of the bay; she was stranding herself. Adem thought now was the time.

"Shoot her! Dose her now!" he hollered.

Michaels pressed the button on his com.

"Tranc teams one, two, three: Fire!" The soldiers, resembling tiny army men from the lookout point with massive tranquilizer guns, began firing, raining down bee-sting-like shots on her.

"It will take the darts 15 seconds to inject the full dose," Adem said into the radio. Sensing her time was up, she began heaving her body further ashore and snapping her jaws at anything she could reach, rows of teeth gyrating. The power and mass of her body were annihilating everything in her path. The temporary island fort was assembled last week, and its 150 inhabitants were destroyed within minutes.

"If anything is going to happen, it will be immediate." Evelyn continued holding out hope for the safety of the tower. It was then that she saw another prominent figure on the radar imaging.

Grabbing the intercom, Evelyn wailed, "Here comes another one!"

"Another what?" Michaels hollered. "Hold your fire," he commanded. They watched their nemesis flip, writhe, and fight as seconds ticked by. Suddenly, one canister emptied, dosing her, and they all began to release. An ear-splitting, otherworldly screech filled the skies. Her back arched. She gave one powerful, epic contortion and then began to glaciate. The wind howled as they observed the cryogenic freeze starting in her body's middle. She thrashed her head and tail convulsively until she turned into a solid mass, with strange popping sounds echoing as she transformed into a block of ice. The sound shifted from an ear-piercing screech to an echo as her eyes glazed over, and her head froze in an upright position. The team suddenly faced an incredible prehistoric sculpture, which seemed impossible. A second beast crashed into the bay, shocking everyone back into action.

"Shoot her! Give it everything you've got!" Adem directed over the radio.

"Full throttle!" Michaels commanded, signaling with his arms for those without an earpiece. With that, harpoons and guns began blazing at will, some bouncing off and others hitting their targets. One arrow struck the frozen monstrosity, causing her to shatter. The second beast was quickly tethered from six angles, and the group watched as they held her precariously like a cat in the cradle. What now?

"Release the thermonuclear!" Torres ordered over her comm.

"Nukes?" Adem yelled. The gigantessa thrashed and keeled over, knocking out the last two towers and the observation deck, causing men and women to be flung perilously to their doom.

The observation deck was struck by a lashing fin, causing it to buckle in the center and toss its occupants, scattering them in every direction. Those who landed on the rocks were dashed and killed. Before Adem knew which direction he was flying, he was underwater, saline filling his lungs. Struggling, he swam toward the shimmering light of the water's surface.

He felt something drift past him, brushing

him ever so gently as fire flashed above them. He saw Evelyn's lifeless body sinking below, unconscious, with bleeding contusions. As the water whipped around him, mirroring the chaos above, she became lodged between two boulders. He pumped his arms and legs with all his might, swimming downward. His fingers grasped the edge of her life jacket as the exertion used up his last breath. With a frantic jerk, he freed her from the rocks. Eyes on the light, he watched more explosions detonating above. He swam with all his strength, finally breaking the surface. He was amazed at how far they were from the island. Shaking her lifeless body, she reanimated, gasping and coughing up water.

"There you go, Darling," he encouraged, towing her by the vest. Wet hair plastered to her face, she sputtered, coughing as the air hit her face. He reached up, moving the strangling mask of hair away from her airway. She was burned and battered with oozing lacerations. Surprised that he had fared so well right next to her, he took to examining himself and noticed just as much damage. *Thank you, endorphins,* he mused, grimacing as the pain began to surface. He paddled, towing her as long as his strength would allow. *To where?* he wondered. *Away,* he rationalized. *But to where?* he asked himself.

In his mind, he recalled the map of the Banda Arc and thought he remembered a freckling of tiny islands surrounding the Arc. Pulling his left arm out from under her neck, lifting her onto his chest, he noticed the flesh sagging from his arm, turning white due to lack of blood flow. In his mind, he had a flash of raising his arm to shield his face as he turned, tucking his wife under his protective wing, feeling the hair on the back of his head singe before they were submerged under warm, torrential water.

They were far from shore now. On the horizon, he could see a colossal fire burning from where they'd come. He couldn't hear any sounds from people or animals and saw no murderous sharks. In fact, he couldn't hear anything at all. Deaf. Well, at least he had his sight.

Dizzy and in deep water, knowing they may be the only moving targets, he decided maybe they should float. He stopped trying to swim actively and turned onto his back. He wriggled downward into the vest, the straps pulling tight under his arms so it would support his head like a pillow. He pulled Evelyn higher up onto his chest. It was a good thing he dwarfed her. He allowed his feet to float upward, becoming buoyant, and used the life jacket to ride the current like a raft, surprised at how quickly they were being swept away from the scene. He tied the straps of her life jacket to his to keep her face above water as long as he remained afloat on his back.

Alarmed by the lack of salt in the water, he swallowed. It tasted almost entirely fresh. He worried about who the survivors were and how many more beasts might be lurking. That was the last thought before he lost consciousness, reaching for his wife. The two floated away on the freshwater sea, seemingly the only two survivors of the last stand.

CHAPTER THIRTY-THREE

Bird's Eye View

ON THE COAST OF NEW YORK CITY, Delsin and Chris sat on the roof of the four-story library, barefoot, feet dangling in the warm, brackish ocean water. The city was quiet and already evacuated. Delsin had sent his family back to the rez. They'd chosen to spend their last days in ceremonial prayer, hoping to reconnect with the land. He had to consider that they might survive inland. The two vowed to do their best to restore harmony and carry out his message if they were lucky enough to survive. The grid was down in this region. Domestic and wild animals scurried unattended in areas still above water. Homo sapiens were a rare sight. The two men sat together in unguarded companionship.

They spoke, voices echoing, bouncing around the architecture of high-rises, eerily devoid of life. They retraced events in their childhoods and shared their hopes, dreams, and achievements in this lifetime. They spoke about what they hadn't gotten to do in this world, exploring their regrets.

"I wish I hadn't wasted time disgracing my ancestors by being so destructive," Delsin said.

Chris grimaced, sympathizing with Del's lament. Then he smiled mischievously.

"Have you ever had a girlfriend?" Chris asked him pointedly, one eyebrow up.

"Yes!" Delsin drawled out, laughing. "Wait. Have you?"

"No!" answered Chris, baldly, shaking his head. "And now, I'm going to die a virgin," he confessed, head hanging, loneliness weighing heavily on his shoulders. They looked at each other soberly. Chris was the first to crack a smile, and they both burst into laughter.

"Don't you believe that you're like earning gold coins in heaven or something?" the young man asked of the priest.

“Oh, I don’t know,” Chris admitted. "Earlier in my life I was certain that it was the right thing to do. I felt for many years that I had a relationship with God. I believed I was on a divine path. Now, knowing it’s all over and seeing all these crazy things that the Bible never talked about, I can’t say with confidence what is to come.” Delsin’s head bobbed in understanding as they both stared out over the sparkling water.

“A shark. I thought we had figured that much out," Delsin said idly.

“Well, yes!” Chris said incredulously, shrugging. “A shark is definitely coming, but I mean the afterlife and all. I can’t say that I’m not afraid to die. I feel that I’ve been a good person and I think I’ve been honorable even if I’ve lost my faith. Will I be condemned for that?" He pondered, nodding his head up and down. "Yes. In the church's eyes, most definitely," he concluded.

"I'm not asking you what your church would say. I'm asking you what you think. I can tell that you are good," Delsin assured him. "Your god knows that." Delsin put his arm around Chris's shoulder, and they both sat there contemplating their mortality. Not only their own, but the passing of their whole species and the world as they know it. As they commiserated, the devastation of the world now upon them, they could clearly see ahead.

They spoke of the decimation happening worldwide: the mudslides, the tornadoes, the volcanic eruptions, the floods, the fires, the diseases, and all the people who had already died. There is a time when all dominant species fall from their throne to the bottom of the food chain. Man has surpassed that time. Through science, technology, and industry, mankind has become too powerful: godlike. Maybe this entity was sent here by God to kill a god, the human race. It was time, they agreed.

Time to lay down and give thanks for our species' time in this realm. As the two men shared their thoughts on the matter, a massive fin broke the surf heading toward them. They continued their conversation as she turned and swayed in the swell, weaving back and forth playfully. A sense of peace enveloped them as their inevitable doom approached.

As she neared the coast, the water began to lap excitedly at their calves, agitated by the tremendous water. They sat in solidarity, knowing that their end was near. As she swam, gracefully coming ever closer, Chris reached out for Del. She was close now.

Her jaw began to open, revealing her red throat, with budding rows of pearly serrated blades. She was absolutely massive, jaws rotating on toothy rows, mowing back and forth in alternating directions, a chainsaw. Just as the figment of their visions drew close enough for them to see her nostrils flare, they heard an ear-piercing sound from the sky. Looking up, they saw a projectile materialize from above. Delsin smiled at the comical whistling sounds as if they were watching a cartoon. It fell as if in slow motion. The two friends closed their eyes and leaned into each other as the bomb fell, made impact, and detonated. Delsin swallowed hard, hearing a roaring wall of water coming toward them. His Adam's apple rose slowly but failed ever to descend.

In the time it takes for a single electrical impulse to contract and relax, triggering one heartbeat, the blue sky turned white, and their world fell silent. As the device hit the sea, the explosion drew in millions of gallons of water, forming a massive crater so powerful that it absorbed everything, including the sound. Seconds later, an explosion unseen by the human eye began rippling outward. Just as quickly, the suction reversed, and starting with a small ring, the impact wave spread out, growing stronger with a pulse like a sonic boom. In an instant, the men were destroyed. Anything within sight, then within a day's drive, and even further away, was obliterated.

The swimming entity, all-wise and knowing, with no emotional attachment to its exterior shell, was reduced to a molecular level. The matter that had made up her body and mind was dispersed over several miles, comprising marine water, buildings, boats, cars, the prophets of Mother Nature, and untold numbers of other life forms. As quickly as it rose, this fountain of dissolution rained violently back down on the Earth, further destroying everything it touched.

At ground zero, the infinydon, the ocean, and all living beings were wiped out of existence. The impact radius expanded, obliterating everything within the forcefield. The two men simply vanished from this plane in the blink of an eye. They left their bodies instantly, with the peace of mind that their time was over: their small flames extinguished. The blast continued for hundreds of miles, destroying flora and fauna along its path. At the same time, it spread through North and Central America, with its force gradually weakening as it reached other continents, causing a global upheaval.

A massive tidal wave swept Adem and Evelyn onto an uninhabited tropical island, waterlogged and unconscious. They lay there, half-drowned from the explosion's impact. The disintegrated remains of the colossus began to draw closer together over time, slowly but surely, floating instinctively back into contact. Globules of the prehistoric monster found each other as if attracted by a magnetic force. Over months, they formed a harmless, embryonic, viscous state. With their mission complete, they drifted back down into the vast ocean's depths to sleep until awakened by Father Time at the next central turning point in evolution. The Earth, now deserted, was left to recover and heal.

CHAPTER THIRTY-FOUR

Elysium

~ One Year Later ~

A LEAN, OLIVE-SKINNED, shaggy-haired Adem hurried back toward camp. His eyes constantly searched the lush landscape for his woman, who was last seen gathering fruits and nuts for their evening meal.

"The sun!" he cried out. "I can see the sun on the horizon!" Over the past year, fallout had shadowed the planet, with fierce, angry clouds darkening the sky; tropical storms had battered them relentlessly. Vegetation had suffered. The couple worried that their time of abundance in this paradise might be coming to an end. If the sun failed to emerge, they believed all the world would perish.

For the initial months, violent storms and tidal waves destroyed their shanty, making their work endless. Most days of the year, there were earthquakes and hurricane-force winds. Over time, the storms started to lessen.

With his wife beside him, he followed the glow of the celestial body through the thinning mists, running in wildling attire to the jungle's edge. They watched in reverence, toes spread wide in the damp sand, holding each other as they witnessed the beautiful, fiery sun setting in the west. They continued to observe the sun until the haze returned, obscuring the night sky. They remained seated comfortably in a cozy nest made from a smooth beach tree trunk behind them, listening to the surf and the calls of evening jungle creatures. From what they could tell, it seemed they were the only human survivors of the catastrophe. Their emergency radios showed no signs of life, and they never encountered any seafarers. For their species' sake, they clung to the hope that some groups had survived, even though they lacked any concrete evidence.

Initially, they were fortunate to have some basic tools in their packs to start fresh. Soon after, they found pieces of wood and other items washed ashore from nearby islands.

Initially, they built a temporary lean-to, but the wind destroyed it. They recovered the lumber to build a sturdier shelter, which they called the ramada because it had a proper roof supported by posts and beams, along with an attached porch that provided comfortable protection. Luckily, they were surrounded by lush tropical gardens that supplied them with healthy plants and animals. Farming was unnecessary; they set traps for protein when needed and sourced vital nutrients from nearby nuts and beans. While out walking, they collected eggs.

As the days went by, they worried less about rescue and instead enjoyed a peaceful harmony with the animals. As the weather warmed, Adem decided to expand the shelter. Evelyn recommended building upward rather than outward to reduce their impact. They used barrels to collect freshwater. Soon, they established a routine of falling asleep at sunset and waking at dawn. Any waste they produced was compostable.

As days blurred into weeks, seasons matured and faded. Over time, the sun shone more often. Flowers blossomed, clear and crisp rains fell, floodwaters receded, and marine life began to recover. The lovers found solace in this strange land as the earth regenerated itself. They grew strong and flexible, learning the ways of this new world, with their shelter shielding them from the jagged edges of the wild.

The planet's devastating injuries matured from open wounds into tough, painful scabs beneath which she stitched herself back together. These crusts eventually softened and, with healing, fell away. Her scars grew from angry, swollen abrasions to shiny, tight seams, which visually told her story. They narrated the epic of a victorious struggle after which Mother Earth thrived. In this quiet, the island became a peaceful, beautiful sanctuary and their home became a cozy refuge.

Following the land's example, the animals thrived. The human’s shelter transformed into semi-outdoor living spaces, featuring collapsible doors that could be opened or closed, although they were typically left open. As they prospered, their shelter consisted of a simple living area, a designated space for preparing food, and a cozy loft for sleeping, which was protected from large animals, although only small rodents were observed. Adem constructed an impressive crow's nest, allowing them to overlook the ocean and spot approaching storms.

The scientists gained a thorough understanding of the land and sea. From their observations, they noted that the water was becoming less saline and were pleased to see marine life rebounding. They set up simple traps in the bay and eventually began catching fish. It took weeks to catch their first small, insignificant meal, but by the end of spring, their supply was plentiful. Each day, they ate nourishing plants using a cut-and-come-again approach, harvesting parts of the plants while leaving most of the plant and root system intact, allowing continuous growth and reharvesting.

Life was peaceful, and they flourished alongside the land. Their quality of life happily improved. No longer fighting for survival, they spent more time exploring the jungle, marveling at life's wonders, and observing diverse wildlife. They learned about their neighbors, including leopards, flocks of birds, red wolves, crocodilians, pythons, large cats, and giant monitor lizards. The felines kept their distance, but they had caught glimpses of them while foraging deep in the forest.

A few sun-dappled pythons had slithered harmlessly through their camp, while others were seen lounging in the trees. The couple discussed whether the animals were becoming less wary of them or if they had become more adept at spotting them. They concluded it was probably a bit of both.

Evelyn was pleased when a specific canine

began lurking around their base. Her pack was observed living near the cliffs. A curious female wolf, which Evie named Kailani, showed interest in the people.

During spring, she grew distant as she cared for her litter of pups. When she returned, one pup became notably bolder. After weeks of playful teasing, he finally took some fish from Evelyn's hand, grabbed it, and ran away skittishly. Evelyn couldn't help but laugh. Following that encounter, he stayed away for a week but eventually reappeared, watching from afar and gradually approaching.

By late spring, he started visiting them every day, quietly observing these peculiar two-legged primates. They would give him scraps and speak softly. One day, he meekly asked for food. This marked the start of Adem's routine of morning fishing and leaving a snack for himself. In the peak of summer, the couple discovered he had camped with them overnight. That night, she named him Nyx and declared him her dog. He was red with a black muzzle and paws.

Two bird species moved into their fort, scavenging crumbs, sometimes even accepting hand-feeding. One was a large flock of flame-breasted sunbirds. Although mainly nectivores, they showed an interest in the activities of these new bipedal creatures. Evelyn enjoyed the large, sweet-smelling flowers growing nearby thanks to their water stores. Songbirds chirped and sang, greeting the dawn. Evie found the soft music and the colorful display of a small, plump sparrow, with a sturdy bill, white cheeks, orange feet, and tangerine-colored bellies, delightful.

They made a charming alarm clock.

One of Adem's favorite animals was the Sunda sambar deer. These large, dark, long-haired deer had antlers, wide-set ears, and shiny, innocent-looking eyes. They lived in small herds and were initially very shy. The surprise came when a herd entered their camp early one morning, and an antlered stag startled the visitors by honking loudly as they entered the clearing. They were quiet, secretive creatures in the wilderness until their breeding season began.

During this period, formidable stags would fight on their hind legs, producing strange and screaming calls. The does would also stomp and rear, hitting other animals with their heads if threatened. After one such fierce tussle, Evelyn noticed a doe with a bright red bald patch on her chest that she took to be an injury. She soon spotted other females with the same mark and suspected disease. Later, she realized that the does with these reddish markings had calves on the ground and were nursing their young.

When tiny, wobbly-legged toddlers appeared in the fawning season, Evelyn started feeling the exhilaration of renewal, mixed with a pang of sadness that they would never be blessed with offspring. Evelyn was delighted to see one mother doe with twins. She realized she hadn't experienced her menses in several weeks? *How many weeks?* she wondered. She really had lost track of time. She put a hand on her flat belly, bewildered.

The days grew longer, and the couple grew comfortable on the island. The land flourished, the crisis abating. The sky continued to clear, seeds germinated, and the jungle bloomed once more, teeming with life. Numerous large, healthy fruits hung from the trees. Reptiles, wildfowl, and mammals all enjoyed the abundance.

Over time, the husband and wife established a nightly routine: walking to the shore after dinner to watch the sunset. They admired the vibrant pastel colors swirling in the sky, creating a breathtaking scene as the day drew to a close. Listening, they observed the world slowly transitioned into night, with insects and amphibians waking up and singing in harmony to lull the creatures of the day to sleep.

One of these evenings, in the crux of her husband's lap, without warning, Evelyn felt a quickening in her belly, a barely perceptible flurry. Her lips quirked at the gentle foreign sensation. Adem, who knew her better than she knew herself, smiled as he reached over and put his rough hand across her exposed midriff.

"I think I'm-,"

"Of course, you are," he responded matter-of-factly.

"How did you know?" she asked, turning.

"You haven't bled in too long, which has been nice. You were making a dreadful mess," he remarked. She pushed him into the sand, smiling. "-and we've had ample time for recreation this year," he drawled, eyebrows raised.

Yes, but I've lost weight. I thought I stopped ovulating because of the stress," she explained.

He reached out and said, "Stress? You're healthier, more relaxed, and in better shape than ever. You're lean, yet muscular, not underweight. I suspect your past infertility was due to stress," he speculated. "I've considered whether I want a boy or a girl, but I've decided it doesn't matter. I want a small person made from us with whom to share our lives." Her eyes widened in surprise and admiration.

"Really?" she asked softly, pressing her cheek into his chest, feeling completely safe and loved.

"I do," he said as he gave her hip a squeeze and kissed the side of her head. "Maybe we should follow Kailani's example and have a whole litter." He mused quietly as the warm darkness fell, gently blanketing them.

"Do you think we are the only lucky ones?" she asked, heartache thick in her voice. "What did we do to deserve another chance while everyone else was lost?"

"It wasn't up to us. So, don't feel guilty. Be glad. We're here. We're alive against all odds, and we're thriving. That's nature. That's life." He responded simply

"You really are a scientist to the core," she reveled. He shrugged, not arguing her point. "Since we are just animals, how many generations of our species do you think have come before us?" she asked him.

"Mmm… I'd guess it's fewer than 500 and now, here comes one more!" he proclaimed, growling with pride.

"Yes, my beast. We will create at least one more." Hopeful about what lies ahead, Adem and Eve, standing alone in the moment, walked back home hand-in-hand through their lovely garden of redemption. The three were on a journey to restore humanity—a kinder, wiser species in harmony with the earth once more.

The end.

ABOUT THE AUTHOR

Marita Christine Lorbiecke is an award-winning, five-star American author with internationally bestselling works. She was raised surrounded by books and inspiring minds, especially her mother, who sadly did not live to see her children reach adulthood due to a tragedy. Her mother loved books, was a philanthropist, and had a knack for animals, traits Marita inherited. Growing up in nature, she developed a deep love for wildlife of all kinds and married with children among a menagerie of exotic animals. Today, Marita and her husband reside on a farm with a private zoo that hosts hundreds of beautiful birds, giant tortoises and lizards, massive snakes, marsupials, and miniature livestock. She has extensive experience as an educator in both public schools and online. Marita attended college in New Mexico, earning multiple degrees, including a Master's. In her spare time, she works as a professional belly dancer, model, and snake wrangler. A true romantic, she is happily living her dream life with her husband, the real Dr. Humbolt, John D Lorbiecke.

EPIGRAPH

ONE HUNDRED LOVE SONNETS: XVII

BY PABLO NERUDA: TRANSLATED BY MARK EISNER

I DON'T LOVE YOU as if you were a rose of salt, topaz,
or arrow of carnations that propagate fire:

I LOVE YOU as one loves certain obscure things,
secretly, between the shadow and the soul.

I LOVE YOU as the plant that doesn't bloom but carries
the light of those flowers, hidden within itself, and
thanks to your love, the tight aroma that arose from the
earth lives dimly in my body.

I LOVE YOU without knowing how, or when, or from
where.

I LOVE YOU directly without problems or pride: I love
you like this because I don't know any other way to love,

except in this form in which I am not nor are you, so
close that your hand upon my chest is mine, so close
that your eyes close with my dreams.

Source: The Essential Neruda: Selected Poems (City Lights Books,

LONGORIA

Made in the USA
Coppell, TX
04 March 2026